DAYS OF DANGER:
EMP Survival Series Book 3

JACK HUNT

DIRECT RESPONSE PUBLISHING

ISBN-13: 978-1986597883
ISBN-10: 1986597881

DAYS OF DANGER

Dedication

For my family.

Prologue

Six Months After EMP

The strike on New Hope Springs would occur in the dead of night. Radical militia leader General Frank Shelby and forty-six members of the Texas Defense Force gathered in the harsh humidity of East Texas to carry out the assault. His group had been aware of the high-end doomsday community long before the EMP. He'd watched with piqued interest as plans were drawn up for the $350 million development, funded by silent investors and protected by 13-foot walls. The property sat on 650 acres with 420 underground bunkers to house 1,700 people. He'd chuckled to himself as the owner marketed it as a "5-star playground equipped with DEFCON 1 preparedness" yet filled it with a golf course, a spa, lagoons, running trails, a gun range, a hotel, a chapel, restaurants, retail shops, a fitness club, a village, sports courts, greenhouses and a private airstrip, and then tried to sell off underground condos in the mid six figures.

What might have been a successful venture never took off because unfortunately it relied on two things: people who had lots of money, and people who were willing to part with it before a disaster. Until the EMP few people saw the urgency, so only seventy of the condos were sold and out of those not everyone made it to the location. Of course, their loss was his gain as he was planning on taking it by force.

Camouflaged, wearing ballistic vests and gripping their M4s, they moved silently through the coniferous forest that hedged in the property. The smell of pine lingered in the air. Mosquitoes nipped at their skin. Nothing would distract them. Frank had spent hours, days, weeks performing reconnaissance with his team to ensure that this went off without a hitch. He'd seen the armed security personnel manning the walls and watchtowers. He understood their strengths and weaknesses and was ready to wipe them out if need be. There was no two ways about it — people were going to die. It was inevitable but necessary.

Inching their way closer to the walled compound, Team 1 approached the south wall while Team 2 approached from the east.

"You in position?" Frank asked his brother John Shelby.

"Roger that," his voice crackled over the radio.

The attack was strategically coordinated so that once the C4 charges were planted, snipers would cut down the perimeter guards and then the walls and gate would be blown on the south side. This would allow time for a diversionary assault.

"Take 'em out!" he said over the radio to four snipers. Frank observed intently as the guards in the watchtowers dropped followed by four men on the southern and eastern walls. He raised the remote detonator, smiled and flipped the switch. The explosion echoed, and flames, pieces of rock and smoke billowed in the air before raining down.

"Go, go, go!" Frank bellowed. His team pressed forward with M4s raised unleashing three-round bursts. Once inside the walls they fanned out and emptied magazine after magazine as residents rushed to defend against the twenty-man team. Seconds later another explosion shook the ground to the east causing even more confusion as Team 2 fanned out in combat intervals, moving at a crouch and flanking them from the east side. It was over in minutes. Those that didn't wish to die threw down their weapons and dropped to their knees, fingers locked behind their heads. Others fled into the safety of the underground compound as a last resort. Smoke from the explosives drifted like a ghostly apparition across the courtyard as his men secured those who'd surrendered while he and his brother John approached the phase 3 bunkers, which surrounded a sixteen-acre lagoon. The bunkers were positioned to the north, east and west, and all had tunnels beneath them allowing people to go back and forth without ever coming out. Frank didn't need to look at the map he'd obtained to know what he was dealing with. In fact he probably knew the place as well as anyone who lived inside.

He lowered his rifle and shouted out loud.

"We have twenty-four of your people out here. We will give you to the count of ten to open the doors and come out otherwise I will have my men execute them one at a time. You decide!"

Frank didn't miss a beat as he turned away. There was no worry on his face. He had no emotion when it came to survival. It was black and white with no gray in the middle. Spending time thinking about other people's suffering only led to weakness, and weakness led to mistakes and ultimately that meant death, and he sure as hell wasn't dying because someone wanted to be a pussy. He'd made up his mind a long time ago when he formed the TDF that there was zero room for mercy. Every decision he made even if it was perceived as showing mercy had a specific purpose. He operated with precision and rarely needed to second-guess his decisions. His eyes roamed the faces of survivors. He didn't want to kill these people any more than he wanted to kill his own men. They served a purpose. They were a means to an end — that being survival, freedom and liberty. Frank was well aware that he had those in his circle who saw the militia as nothing more than family. It gave them a sense of belonging, and he had no problem with that. For him though, it was much more. It was about control — it had to be as the government were masters at it. While he hadn't seen them impose martial law, he knew it was only a matter of time until the military returned to the shores, and what remained of government tried to pick up the pieces. The first thing they would try to do was disarm the American people, and there was no chance in hell of that happening.

In order to ride out the next year he had to think beyond his own resources and look at those who had stockpiled their own. New Hope Springs was exactly that. Just another resource that could be used to establish what he'd already built. He could already tell from the pitiful defense shown that these people were lacking.

He glanced at John who tossed him a serious expression. Unlike him, it had taken close to a month before John came around to the realization that if he didn't kill others, they would perish. While Frank had taken every precaution prior to the EMP to create a camp stocked with enough critical provisions to last them a year, they needed to stay ahead of the game and that meant taking action early. Being proactive was vital to survival. It was because of his own early action that he and the others had survived the initial attack on America; and once again it was because of his actions they would take this compound.

John scowled.

Frank responded, "Oh settle down, you know it has to be done."

"To gain entry but we are in now," John replied.

Frank pointed at the bunkers. "We're not in until those doors open up. That's where they have the dry food and ammo stored." He took a deep breath and pulled out a pack of cigarettes from his top pocket. "And, whoever is in charge of this place is inside."

"How can you be sure?"

"Call it a gut instinct," he said sparking up his cigarette while cupping a hand to block the wind. All the while he had been counting down. Once he reached one he turned and gave a nod to Davis, one of his men. Without hesitation Davis aimed the gun and squeezed the trigger. A sharp pop. A man in his early twenties collapsed to the horror of the other survivors.

"Ten more seconds and another one dies. Do you really want their blood on your hands?" Frank yelled.

He had no idea whether they would open and quite frankly he didn't care. One way or another he and his men would get inside. If they were smart, they wouldn't come out. But based on what he saw around him, he'd already concluded he wasn't dealing with bright individuals. Frank didn't bother shouting out the numbers, he wasn't into theatrics. Silence was much more effective. It could eat away at a man. John looked at him again with an expression of concern before Frank gave the go-ahead for a second individual to be killed.

Three people had to die before the door cracked open and the asshole in charge emerged.

The man was an athletic-looking fella, with deep-set brown eyes, a full head of hair. Frank approached him and walked around him the way a lion might examine its prey before pouncing. "You in charge?"

He nodded. "That's right."

"What's your name?"

"Ryan Hayes."

Frank squinted then shook his head.

"You're not in charge. Where is he?"

Ryan shrugged. "I'm not sure what you're on about. I'm responsible for those here."

"Then why were you never mentioned in the development?"

"I was."

Frank ambled toward him and got eye-to-eye. "Don't bullshit me."

"I'm not."

Without missing a beat, he grabbed the man by the back of the neck and thrust him down on the ground. He coughed hard as Frank backed up and raised his M4 at his head.

"Come on out, Harlan Jacobs, or I will kill him," Frank yelled.

"Stop!" a voice cried out. "Enough killing."

From among the crowd that was beginning to stream out of the bunker an older man in his late fifties elbowed his way to the front. Frank waited until he was within arm's reach then he backhanded him. "Sending out someone to act on your behalf." He tutted. "That's cowardly." He breathed in deeply and his eyes washed over those inside. "Okay, so this is how it's going to work. Everything you have is still yours. That's right, except for one caveat. You are no longer in charge of it, we are. Do I make myself clear or do I need to provide a demonstration?"

Harlan shook his head and wiped blood from his lip as Frank gazed down at him.

"Good, well then how about you give us a tour of this place?"

Chapter 1

Saranac Lake

Seven Days Later

Elliot gritted his teeth as the Katana sword cut into his hand. Blood trickled down his wrist as he struggled to get the hefty man off him. The attack was lightning fast — he didn't have a chance to escape — and the one exit in the Wild Outfitters store was now blocked by a toppled steel cabinet. Shutters covered windows, and the only daylight seeped in from a thin band around the edges of the metal.

"Gary!" he shouted but got no response. He didn't know if he was dead or just unconscious. One hour earlier, he, Gary, Damon and Jesse had arrived in the town located just twenty minutes northwest of Lake Placid. After six months of eating their way through

19

supplies and struggling to find wildlife in the surrounding forest, they'd returned to scavenging. Every two days they would search homes locally or travel to surrounding towns in the county.

It had been a crap shoot so far with minimal luck in finding anything. Raiders had already swept through the town's grocery and pharmacies, leaving very little behind. Owners or gangs guarded the few remaining untouched stores. He and Gary spotted a store that sold items for folks looking to survive in the wilderness and figured they'd see what it might offer — big mistake. Unlike most of the valuable stores, hotels and restaurants guarded by groups of armed men, this one just had a warning sign out front.

Drool dripped from the bearded man's lips. His eyes were dark and wild, and his hair long and unruly. He sneered and was using all of his strength to push down the blade. There was no doubt in Elliot's mind that if he released his grip, the Katana would slice through his neck. Fortunately the blade itself wasn't as sharp as it should have been otherwise it would have cut through his hand like butter. Still, with blood dripping down his arm, it didn't mean that it wouldn't happen.

"We didn't know there was anyone in here," Elliot cried out, hoping to reason with him — an utterly pointless attempt — he wasn't having any of it. He was dressed in a thick plaid shirt, torn jeans and camo boots. He smelled like he hadn't bathed in months. The stench alone was overwhelming.

"Didn't you see the sign?" he bellowed back.

He would have responded, but he was using all his strength to hold him at bay. Elliot's arms trembled, and he cried out as the blade cut deeper. Any further and it was liable to sever ligaments in his hand. He winced and shouted again for Gary.

Right then a dark mass came into view off to his left. Within seconds it was over as Gary cracked the guy over the head with a baseball bat. His body slumped to one side and Elliot crawled out from underneath as Gary followed through with a few more strikes to make sure he wasn't getting up again.

Wood hitting bone was a horrid sound.

"Gary, I think he's dead," Elliot said grabbing his arm to stop him from striking again. Having been inside that store for close to ten minutes, most of which had been spent fighting off their assailant, his eyes had now adjusted. Gary looked like he was in a state of shock and bewilderment. He nodded a few times and backed up giving Elliot a clear view of the bloody carnage. The man's face had been reduced to pulp.

Both of them were exhausted as they staggered back and Gary braced himself against the counter. It was hard to know if the guy was the owner or whether he was just squatting. There was a sleeping bag rolled out behind the counter with a book, a porno mag, a few red apples and a crank-up lamp.

"Let's grab what we can and get out of here."

"You were right, Elliot," Gary said without even looking at him.

"About?"

"Everything. I was a fool to think that I could have maintained order."

There was a pause.

"You did what you thought was best," Elliot replied.

"So did you but you could see it, couldn't you?"

Elliot shrugged. "It doesn't matter. All that matters is survival now."

"It does because I wasted all that time digging my heels into the ground wanting to believe that we were better than this — that we were more than savages but that's what we are, aren't we?"

"Fight or flight, my friend. It's the basic instinct we all have. Tear away the infrastructure that we rely on and people will revert back to what is hard-wired within them."

Elliot exhaled hard and scooped up the flashlight he'd dropped. He switched it on and a bright beam of white light bathed the room. He removed his baseball cap and wiped beads of sweat from his brow while eyeing what remained in the store. Surprisingly it hadn't been looted.

Six months. It was astonishing but then again… he glanced at the man. He had put up one hell of a fight. Perhaps that Katana sword wasn't so sharp for a reason.

"This place should have been empty by now."

Gary didn't reply. He pulled out a pack of cigarettes and lit one. An old habit that he'd resumed a few months ago because of the stress he'd been under. Gary had become a very different man in six months. After multiple attacks on their lives, the death of Ted Murphy and the subsequent death of Mayor Hammond who lived another two months before being savagely beaten to death — Gary had thrown in the towel on attempting to protect the town. Many people were out of control and those that weren't either had fled or no longer wanted to risk their neck for others.

"We're going to have to leave Lake Placid," Gary blurted out as Elliot loaded up a black bag with a four-man tent, two sleeping bags and numerous camping tools.

"What?"

Gary turned and took a hard drag on his cigarette. It

glowed a bright orange in the darkness. Elliot cast the light in his direction and shadows danced against his features.

"You've seen it. We can't survive here any longer. Hell, I don't think we can make it through another winter. The last one was brutal."

Elliot stopped filling the bag as he could tell he was serious. That was one thing he knew about Gary — he rarely proposed anything unless he meant it. Maybe that's why Elliot had accepted his apology six months ago.

Elliot ran a hand over his face and said, "It's bad. I admit it but we've made it this far, Gary."

"And we've drained our resources. There is nothing left in the bunker. We've barely managed to scavenge enough cans of food over the past month and hunting… well…" he scoffed. "That's a joke. No, I can't keep doing it, Elliot."

"Is this about Jill? Rayna said she'd voiced her concern."

He furrowed his brow. "No." He paused for a second.

"Okay, maybe. Look, she has a point, Elliot. I mean, we've traveled to nearly every town in Essex County. You've seen it yourself. It's bad. We're lucky to have made it this long without losing our minds or starving to death."

"But we've planted seeds."

"And that's going to take time to grow."

"So, in the meantime we keep doing what we've been doing," Elliot said turning back to the task at hand. He didn't want to linger in the store too long. The key was to get in and out fast. Every town was different. Some were barren and deserted — those were the smaller towns that didn't offer much. As for the rest? Well, they were run by gangs or locals who would fight tooth and nail to hold on to what they had. He couldn't blame them. They were doing the same. No one wanted to die. People had mouths to feed, kids to clothe. Some towns had reverted back to trading, but that only worked if folks were civil and desperate times didn't nurture civil behavior.

Gary exhaled hard. "It's not going to work. Even if we

could scrape together enough to ride out another six months, what then? If one of us becomes sick over the winter, how are we going to cope?"

Elliot dropped the bag and stared at his old friend. "It's not going to be any better out there, Gary. If we're struggling so is everyone else. The grass is never greener on the other side."

"I beg to differ. You heard the radio broadcast about FEMA camps."

Elliot scoffed. "You want to lay down your gun and walk into a prison?"

"Those prisons have food, military, doctors, medicine."

"And they have people who want to control."

"It worked before the fall, didn't it?"

He couldn't argue with that. Sure, there was a lot that was wrong about society before the EMP but it functioned, even if it infringed on people's liberties. But that was then, this was now.

Elliot shook his head. "Nah, it's too big a risk. Who

would hold them responsible if they got a god complex?"

"Who holds any of us responsible?" Gary shot back.

"Sure but at least out here we call the shots."

Gary crushed his cigarette below his boot. "If society managed to crawl its way back to something that resembled what it was before the EMP, you would have to toe the line then. I get a sense this isn't as much about calling the shots as it is about having others tell you what to do."

"Is that a bad thing?" Elliot asked.

"You had no problem with it in the military."

Elliot scoffed then smiled. "You always have an answer for everything, don't you? C'mon, stop yakking and give me a hand." He went back to filling the bag. "I hope Damon has managed to find something worthwhile as this won't fill bellies."

* * *

"Um, this tastes fine," Damon said smiling from ear to ear as he smacked his lips. "Would you like an extra muffin with that coffee, sir?" Damon said in a posh voice as he tossed Jesse another chocolate chip muffin inside a clear package. The quaint little café called Origin Coffee was located on Main Street. To get inside they climbed a fire escape at the rear of the three-story building and broke a window on the second floor. Once inside the apartment they made their way down a narrow staircase and broke through a flimsy door to gain entry to the cafe. Now they sat in a storage area out back devouring a box full of muffins. They weren't exactly fresh but damn they tasted good.

Jesse turned the muffin in his hand. "To think they didn't even make their own."

"Oh I'm sure they did, but they had to have a backup plan."

He snorted looking around. "I can't believe someone hasn't broken into this place. Coffee's still in high demand." He took a sip of a cold brew they'd whipped together using bottled water and ground beans from sealed bags.

"Nah, someone has been in here, they were just clever

enough to make it look as if it had already been ransacked."

Outside the front of the store, coffee makers had been smashed on the ground and a section of the steel shutters had been peeled back to reveal a cracked window. Inside, wooden chairs and round tables were piled against the window, and twisted together to make it virtually impossible for someone to enter. However, someone had entered and was still using the property, as they'd found several boxes of muffins already open.

"You know we should probably save some of these for the others."

"Probably," Damon said, his lip curling up as he opened another one. Food was scarce and creature comforts like chocolate were a luxury.

Jesse stopped chewing. "Why didn't they take the box?"

"What?" Damon replied distracted as he eyed blueberry muffins in another box.

"Well, if someone has been using this place, wouldn't

it make sense to take everything back to your home?"

"Not if this is your home," he replied pointing up to the apartment above. There were two apartments; one above the café and one more above that, at least they assumed it was another apartment. They'd entered the second one but hadn't explored the rest. "My guess — they're out."

Jesse nodded and grabbed up his Glock and headed toward the door.

Damon frowned. "Where are you going?"

"To check out the other apartment."

"Hold up." He scrambled to his feet taking one more bite before tossing the rest back into the box. Jesse had been hesitant to scavenge since his close brush with death two months ago. They'd been doing the exact same thing as they were today, searching for food and supplies and trying to avoid what he felt was the inevitable — death. Two months ago they'd entered Elizabethtown and divided up so they could cover more ground. While they came away from that trip with lots of supplies, it didn't come without a cost. He'd been ambushed by four guys and beaten within an inch of his life. If Damon hadn't heard the commotion and shot one of them, he was certain he wouldn't have survived. To say that it had shaken him would have been an understatement. He was nervous about entering towns and since that day they made a rule to stick together in twos even if it meant they couldn't cover as much ground. It was safer than going alone.

Jesse raised the Glock as he approached the door to the third-story apartment. He put his ear to the wood and listened for movement inside. Nothing. There was no sound. He put a hand on the knob and gave it a twist but it was locked.

"We can use the fire escape around back," Damon said trudging back down the steps.

"You think you could make more noise?" Jesse said, noticing how he was dragging his feet. He smiled.

"Relax, there is no one here."

"Famous last words," Jesse said, his lip curling up.

They weaved around furniture in the second apartment and climbed back out onto the black fire escape.

"So I notice things are heating up between you and Maggie," Damon said leading the way.

Jesse raised an eyebrow. "And?"

He shrugged and pulled a face. "Nothing. I'm just making small talk."

"It wouldn't be because you're jealous, would it?"

"Jealous? Of you and Maggie? Please. That gal has issues."

"And you don't? I'm pretty sure you were the one that did time inside."

"Not my fault."

"Isn't that what they all say?" Jesse shot back. Damon went quiet as they climbed the final flight of steps and reached the window to the next apartment. Damon ran a hand over the pane of glass. A thick layer of dust had gathered.

"So?" Jesse asked.

"Seems like we are in luck." Damon reared back his elbow and shattered the glass before crawling inside. Glass crunched beneath their boots as they entered the quiet abode. There really wasn't much to it — a couch, two modern-style armchairs, a brick fireplace with family photos on the mantel, a tiny kitchen and two rooms out back. Damon picked up a photo and glanced at it.

"Now that's a hot-looking girl," he said tossing it to Jesse.

He chuckled. "She's way out of your league."

"And you would know because?"

"C'mon, look at you, Damon. I'm guessing you dressed and smelled this way before the EMP."

"I'll have you know—"

Before he could spit the words out, they heard movement. It was almost inaudible and for a second he wasn't sure he'd heard anything. Damon eyed Jesse and put a finger up to his lips then pulled his Glock and headed towards the tight corridor that went down to the two other rooms.

Chapter 2

Harlan Jacobs cowered in the corner as militia rifled through their supplies taking whatever they damn well pleased. He wasn't prepared for this. There was no rule book on how to handle being ambushed. Sure, he'd hired armed personnel and done his homework on what New Hope Springs required in order to satisfy the needs of the desperate, but he didn't bank on facing these kinds of individuals.

After all, he was just a businessman who had seen an opportunity and taken it. Four years before the EMP he'd heard through the grapevine that a company by the name of Atlas Survival Shelters was making an absolute killing selling corrugated pipe shelters all around the world. They'd gone from selling sixty to a thousand a year and were not only raking in profits but doing a lot of good in the process. Up until that point he'd dabbled in different markets, buying and selling products, and had made a good living from it but it had always left him feeling empty. The fact was for all his efforts he never felt satisfied at the end of the day. Business was just a means to an end — to pay bills, give his family what they wanted — and it allowed him to keep up with the Joneses. If he was honest with himself, he'd have to admit he'd spent the better part of the past thirty years chasing what others had just so he didn't feel like such a loser.

"Yep, I think we are going to fit in here just nicely," Frank said while one of his men held a clipboard and took note of every item in storage. He turned his attention to Harlan. "Now I know you're concerned about your family and you're probably wondering how this is all going to work but I want to reassure you. You're in good hands. You did the right thing opening the doors. You see, we would have got in either way." He smiled and returned to giving out commands to his men.

Harlan eyed his wife, Bridget, from across the room. She had pulled their three children in close to her as one of Shelby's men kept a Sig Sauer against her rib cage.

That was the first thing he'd done once they stepped inside. Shelby wanted to be introduced to his family. He should have known he was planning on using them as leverage to get him to hand over the codes to the vault.

Harlan quietly cursed the day he'd had the idea for New Hope Springs.

He wasn't even a resident of Texas but he figured that would be the best place to build due to the good weather, water supply, rural farmland and because the cost to build there was a lot cheaper. At first he'd thought of starting a competing business to Atlas Shelters but then he figured it would be more advantageous to take things to the next level and build a community. If the EMP had never occurred, he would have used the place as a resort for preppers. He'd envisioned it being the number one place in the United States for prepper retreats. He would rent out the bunkers at crazy low prices and then market each one like a timeshare. There was no way he could lose. He managed to sell off a number of the bunkers prior to the EMP and he had no doubt in his mind within two to three years he would have been ready to build another community on the West Coast. He had big dreams, and he thought he'd covered every corner but obviously not.

"Get up, Harlan, take me to your office. I think it's time you and I had a little chat," Shelby said. He rose from the ground where he'd been after Shelby struck him. His knees ached. He rubbed them and scowled.

"And wipe that scowl off your face. If you want things to go smoothly you and I are going to need to come to an agreement. Now let's go. Lead the way."

Harlan led him out of the stockroom and through the maze of underground tunnels that were like laid out like a spider's web. He brought him to a clubhouse on the north side of the property. It was squeezed between the driving range for golfers, a nine-acre lagoon and the spa. All the generators that distributed power used diesel, but the place also ran in conjunction with solar and wind, which meant it didn't require running them for more than a couple of hours before the batteries were charged.

They entered his large office that doubled as a library

and Shelby looked around as he took off his camouflage helmet and took a seat behind the desk.

"While I have to applaud you, Harlan, you did a great job on this place — but, you made a few big mistakes when you envisioned it. You see, guys like you are always trying to impress. You have to do things on a big scale. I mean, let me guess you said to yourself — go big or go home, right?" He laughed. "But that's the problem, you didn't really think about the end game. Now me? When I started my group, we began small and were very picky about who got in. Now I'm guessing you didn't do any background checks on those guys you had on the wall, am I right?"

"Of course I did."

"Then you hired wrong. You see, had I been at the helm of this little enterprise I would have made security the first thing on my list, not the last. You see, all these walls you have built around this place are only as good as your ability to protect them from assaults. Now had you been smart you would have brought in trucks and dumped a shitload of soil and raised this whole community up on a hill. I would have also cleared away a hell of a lot more of the forest. That way you would have seen us coming. But that's neither here nor there," he said looking around. "You got any alcohol?"

Harlan eyed him with a look of disgust. He motioned with his head to a cabinet on the far side of the wall.

"Well, chop-chop, it's not going to jump out of the fucking bottle!" Shelby said, putting his dirty boots up on Harlan's desk and muddying all the paperwork. He reached into his top pocket and pulled out his smokes and lit one. Harlan narrowed his eyes and trudged over to make him a drink. As he pulled the bottle out and turned his back, he thought about the cyanide pills he had in his drawer. He'd bought them for numerous reasons, some of which were self-explanatory. He could slip the contents of one into his drink.

"Harlan, turn this way. I want to see you pouring that drink. I can't have you slipping anything inside."

Bastard! The man was one step ahead. Harlan clenched

his jaw and finished pouring two fingers before handing him a glass.

"Aren't you going to join me?" Shelby asked.

"I'd prefer not."

"Well I would prefer you do." He cocked his head to one side. Shelby let out a laugh while Harlan poured another. "I know what you're thinking. How did I arrive at this point? Well it doesn't matter. All that matters is how you will move forward." He sniffed hard. "Take a seat," he said motioning to a chair. Harlan slumped down cupping the glass with both hands and looking despondently into the golden liquid. He swirled it around a few times before Shelby leaned forward. "Cheers," he said. He waited for Harlan to clink glasses. Reluctantly he did it then watched as Shelby drained his glass. "Oh that is some good shit! What year was that?"

"2000."

He smacked his lips. "Um. Superb. Right, let's get down to business, shall we?"

Shelby took a drag on his cigarette and blew smoke his

way.

"Are you going to harm my family?" Harlan asked.

His brow pinched. "Of course not. We're not animals. We're not the enemy. Let's make something clear right now. Your enemies are ours, and ours are yours. The only ones you need to fear are those North Koreans as I'm pretty damn sure they have a second wave planned for America. Which is why it's important we stick together. I watch your back. You watch mine."

Harlan said nothing.

Shelby sighed and leaned back in the plush leather chair. "Okay, I know you think that we're some radical group but you'd be wrong. You see, we aren't in the business of harming Americans." He paused. "Tell me, you ever heard of the three percenters?"

Harlan shook his head.

"Are you serious?"

Harlan shrugged so Shelby tried to prompt his memory.

"You don't recall three percent of the thirteen colonies

fighting against Great Britain during the American Revolution?"

"No."

He tapped the table with his finger and laughed. "Come on, Harlan. Did you not stay abreast of the news?" He paused for effect. "Okay, look. Let's just say we are kind of like them. We are against attempts at restriction of gun ownership, we believe in our constitutional rights and some might say we consider the government to be... um... tyrannical."

Harlan gave a confused expression. "But?"

Shelby laughed and wagged his finger. "Nothing gets by you, does it, Harlan? Well, besides armed militia but let's not rub salt into wounds." He took another drag of his cigarette and grinned. "I guess what I'm trying to say is we aren't three percenters, but we believe that eventually a war is coming and I'm not talking about those damn Koreans. I'm speaking about our own government. Mark my words. It may not be today, or next month or even a year from now but they will show up and will demand our weapons and demand that we fall in line."

"And… that's bad?" Harlan asked.

"It is if you want your constitutional rights trampled." He dropped his cigarette into the glass and it let out a short hiss in what remained of his drink. "Hell, I wouldn't be surprised if our tax dollars paid for this attack on America."

"You are kidding, right?" Harlan said, unable to believe that someone could be that deluded.

Shelby leaned in and clasped his hands together. He had this dead serious expression on his face. "No. No I'm not. America has been paying Iran millions for years and supplying them with weapons. Now I know some patriots might get all up in arms at the thought that America is in cahoots with Russia or even North Korea but it wouldn't be a first." He leaned back and his eyes roamed the room. "That's why us Americans need to stick together. Work together to build something better. And that all begins here, Harlan, in the great state of Texas."

"If you are so anti-government, why didn't you create your own compound?"

He laughed. "Shit. If I have to answer that you are dumber than I think you are. Think about it, Harlan. Go on. I can see that pea brain of yours is ticking over trying to connect the dots." He gave it a few seconds before he continued. "Okay, I can't bear the suspense. Money. It requires a shitload of money to build something like this and well, why bother approaching investors and meddling in the legality of it all when I have someone like you doing it all for me?"

Harlan stared back at him blankly.

"That's right, I've been watching your enterprise since the very first day local papers got wind of it. I have to say it was smart but like most of these ventures you're so busy catering to people's whims and needs that you overlook the small details. That's why we broke through that wall of yours tonight. Don't act surprised. If it weren't us, it would have eventually been someone else. At least you're still alive."

"I guess I should thank you," Harlan said.

"If you like," he replied before pulling at a couple of the drawers in front of him. He opened two then pulled out a box from a third one. "Um, what do we have here?"

He cracked it open to reveal expensive cigars.

"The Regius Double Corona." He pulled one out and bit off the end and spat it on the floor while eyeing Harlan. "How much?"

Harlan didn't reply.

"Seriously, Harlan. Is this how it's going to be every time we talk?"

There was a pause.

"$52,785.20."

"Holy shit. You fat cats love to spend. I gather that's for the box and not per cigar?"

"That covers a flight to Regius headquarters to create my own blend and receive a thousand."

"Well then I can't wait to try this."

Shelby pulled another one out and tossed it at him. "Here, like I said. What's yours is yours, but I get to control what goes where." He winked then lit the end and twisted it in his thick fingers while eyeing him. The end glowed a hot orange, and the air filled with thick, pungent smoke. "Oh that shit is so sweet and smooth. I've got to say, Harlan. I like how you spend money. Now back to business." He waved his hand around. "What kind of communications technology have you got here?"

"Ham radio."

"That's it?"

"Walkie-talkies."

"Yeah, those worked well." He laughed and took another hit on the cigar. "Now let me think. We have a lot of rooms to fill in this place, and we are going to need a lot more people."

Harlan's brow furrowed. "Why?"

"Dear God, man, have you not been paying attention for the last ten minutes? I recommend you open your ears as I'm not in the habit of repeating myself. We are here to ensure your survival as well as ours. In order to make that work, we need to put the word out, let others know about this place. Call it a friendly gesture."

He frowned and Shelby rolled his eyes.

"What is it, Harlan? What don't you understand?" he said in his most condescending voice.

"But doesn't that defeat the purpose?"

"What purpose?"

"Of taking what we have, if you give it away to others."

Shelby leaned forward. "I didn't say we were going to give it away." He looked up at his brother who was standing by the door. "Did you hear me say anything about giving it away, John?"

"I don't believe I did, brother."

Shelby flashed his pearly whites. "Like I said, Harlan, you need to open your eyes and read between the lines."

"Then why?"

"Yours is not to question why but to…" he clicked his fingers and acted as if he couldn't find the words. "What is it again, John?"

Harlan could tell he was toying with him. Trying to

make him out to be a fool.

"Do or die," John replied.

He jabbed his finger and bit his bottom lip. "That's it. Your place is not to question why, yours is to do or die!"

Chapter 3

Damon tightened his grip on the Glock as he used the tip of his boot to ease open the door to one of the two rooms. Jesse stood across from him. Over the past six months they'd got used to clearing rooms, but it was never easy. He swallowed hard, his pulse racing as he shone the flashlight into the darkened room. Even though it was daylight out, thick drapes made it virtually impossible to see inside without light. He held it in his right hand over the top of his Glock, which was in his left. The light swept across an ordinary-looking room. A bed, a side table, a rocking chair and a sofa filled the cramped space. He jerked his head to the closet and then to the bed without shining the light on them. Jesse nodded and darted into the room raking his gun, he waited as Damon dropped and cast the light beneath the bed. Nothing. A second later he cocked his head and paused to see if he could get a bead on any further movement. Nothing. It was silent, not even the sound of breathing. Jesse slid over to the closet, approaching it from the left side and indicating a countdown before he'd slide it open.

Damon prepared for the unexpected.

Three, two, one. Jesse mouthed the numbers then leaned and slid the door open.

His heart sped up as he scanned the floor.

Nothing — just a woman's shoes, shirts and above that a bookshelf.

They backed up and approached the next room repeating the process over again. This time as they got close to the closet Damon could have sworn he heard breathing.

"Come out! I know you're in there," he bellowed.

No response.

Damon clenched his jaw and with a nod he indicated for Jesse to slide the closet door open. This time, however, he made sure he was off to one side, slightly guarded by the main door.

As the door slid open, a muzzle flashed and gunfire echoed. A round punctured the wall above Damon's head. He was just about to return fire when his flashlight fell upon the face of a young woman. He dropped back behind the door and yelled.

"Whoa! We're not gonna hurt you."

He snuck a peek around the door. "Look, I'm putting my gun in my waistband. It's okay."

He held out the gun, knowing that Jesse was on the ready if anything went wrong.

As he edged out, he kept the light on her. She squinted, and he noted she had wild eyes and dark wavy hair that came down to her shoulders. They reflected back like a cat caught in a spotlight. She had her handgun out, sweeping back and forth between them.

"Just put it down," Damon said.

"Get out!" she yelled.

"We're…"

"I said get out!" She screamed this time.

"Okay. Okay," Damon replied motioning to Jesse, and

they slowly backed out of the room. Outside in the hallway they made their way down the narrow corridor, the woman following close behind. He glanced over his shoulder and recognized her from the photo on the mantel. Good-looking woman. Early twenties. Athletic in appearance. As daylight fell upon her, he got a better look. She was surprisingly clean for someone who had been in an apocalypse for the past six months. She wore dark jeans and a black fitted jacket and had a knife attached to her thigh, and another handgun on her hip. This girl wasn't messing around.

Once they were in the living room, he turned and she yelled again. "Turn away!"

"Where are your parents?" Damon asked looking back again.

She glared. "What?"

"I saw the photo on the mantel," he said motioning with his head. He could tell she wasn't a threat otherwise she would have killed them by now. She'd had plenty of opportunities. Maybe that's why he ignored her third attempt at telling him what to do.

"None of your damn business. Now move it." She motioned with the gun towards the shattered window.

"You know being out here all by yourself can't be good."

"I can take care of myself," she replied.

"I can see." He looked at Jesse who was a little pale in the face. He hadn't been the same since his brush with death. It was like whatever backbone he had in him had shriveled up and died. Jesse was the first to climb out of the window onto the fire escape. The girl stuck the gun in Damon's face and screamed for him to hurry up. Under any other conditions Damon might have been inclined to swat the gun out of his face, but she didn't have anything they needed and he sure as hell wasn't going to lose his head over a few boxes of muffins. Jesse started making his way down, his boots clanging against the metal steps. Damon paused and looked back at her.

"You know, not everyone is bad."

She didn't respond, and he didn't have any intentions

of engaging any further. He followed Jesse down and they were about to enter the second apartment when she yelled. "No! Keep going down."

"We are, we just need to grab a few things," Jesse said.

"You don't need shit. Now move it!"

Damon chuckled. She was a feisty one but not very smart. Had they been a gang, she would have been raped and dead by now. They'd already seem them roaming the town attacking anyone who had anything of value.

"You know, it's only a matter of time before they show up here."

He didn't need to explain who "they" were. If she'd been living there for a while she must have seen them.

"I'll be ready," the woman replied.

"We're from Lake Placid," Damon said.

"Well then how about you head back there?"

"You can come if you want."

"And why would I do that?"

"Protection?"

"I can handle myself."

"I'm just saying, it's easier to ride this out with friends."

Jesse scowled. "What are you doing?" he muttered.

"Testing the waters."

"But we don't have enough for ourselves," he said in a hushed tone.

"Would you both shut up and get on your way before I change my mind," she said.

They made their way down the ladder and dropped to the ground. Damon looked up at the woman who didn't take her eyes off them until they disappeared around a corner. Jesse continued heading in the direction of the line of stores Elliot and Gary had gone to check out while Damon stood there for a second.

"C'mon, we need to get back to the others before some of those assholes spot us."

He shifted his weight from one foot to the next. "She's by herself, Jesse."

"And? I'm sure there are a lot of people by themselves."

"Nah, something doesn't feel right."

"Oh, I agree," Jesse said before bellowing, "That's because we are standing out in the open like sitting ducks! Now let's go!"

Damon waved him off. "You head on. I'm going back."

"What?" he blurted out, an expression of confusion on his face. "Are you out of your mind? We're lucky to be alive right now."

"She had no intention of killing otherwise I would have been dead by now."

"Perhaps she's a bad shot," Jesse replied.

He shook his head and turned.

"Damon." Jesse grabbed him by the arm.

"Just tell Elliot where I am. I'll join you in ten."

"It's not happening. Where you go, I go."

"Suit yourself. Just keep it down."

They ambled down the alley that went around the side of the building. When they reached the end, Damon cut the corner to see if she was still at the top of the fire escape.

"Listen, stay here," he said while removing his boots. "Watch my six."

Jesse frowned. "What are you doing?"

"Watch and learn."

He hurried out running at a crouch towards the fire escape but instead of going up it, he used the drainpipe at the corner of the building and began climbing. He wanted to make as little noise as possible. It didn't take long to reach the third floor. He inched his way over to the fire escape and clambered across doing his best to stay silent. Staying in a crouched position he made his way to the window and peered in. He couldn't see her but he could hear gentle sobbing.

Damon looked down at Jesse who palmed his face and gestured for him to get down but that wasn't happening — not until he knew. He really wasn't sure why he was risking his neck for someone he didn't know. It wasn't the first time they'd encountered people by themselves. Survivors were out there, and they'd left many behind.

But something about this didn't feel right, or maybe it was the opposite. He glanced down at the broken glass and shook his head. *Shit.* The last thing he needed was a shard embedded or for her to hear. There was a table off to the right of the window with a bunch of computer gear on it. There was no telling how stable it was but he decided to give it a try. He slipped in and reached over with one leg to the table and then did the same with the next. He was certain she would hear him. When he finally managed to lower himself to the floor, the sobbing had stopped. His heart thumped in his chest and he paused waiting for movement, then he heard her crying again. He moved stealthily down the corridor, withdrawing his Glock for protection. There was no telling if her aim would improve this time.

He continued down the corridor and eased the door open on the room they'd found her in. Peering in, he squinted trying to make out where she was. That's when he heard a gun cocking behind his head.

"I told you. I can take care of myself."

Damon's eyes closed. "Shit."

His hands immediately went up.

"Drop it."

He released the gun, and it clattered.

"Where's your dopey ass friend?"

"Outside."

"Better question, where's your boots?"

"Outside."

"Huh! Maybe he's the smart one," she replied.

The next thing he felt was a sharp blow to the back of the head.

* * *

When Damon came to, he could hear the sound of chatter. He groaned and instinctively reached for his skull. It was throbbing hard, and he had one hell of a headache. Light flickered, and he saw the woman sitting in a chair in the living room with Jesse perched on the couch across from her. Both were drinking from china teacups like they were at some fancy tea party.

"Ah, there is he is. I expect you're thirsty," she said in a casual manner.

Damon rubbed the back of his head. "What the hell…"

"She nailed your ass," Jesse explained with a smirk on his face before taking a sip of his drink.

"Did you really have to hit me?"

"I thought it would knock some sense into you. Now your buddy here — he had the right idea. Smart guy."

Jesse looked all pleased with himself.

"Fearful you mean," Damon shot back.

"Fearful, maybe, smart — definitely."

She returned with a cup of hot coffee. He straightened up as he'd been lying down on the sofa. "Ella's the name. And you are?"

Damon coughed. "In pain."

She let out a laugh as he took the cup.

"Is this how you treat all your guests?" he asked.

"Only those that don't listen."

"How long you been living here?"

"About two months. It's my parents' apartment. They

also own the one on the second floor but that was rented out. I was living in Lake George when the lights went out. Made my way back and…" She trailed off looking over at the framed photo on the mantel before dropping her head.

"Did you find them?" Damon asked.

"Yeah. I did. Buried them out back."

He nodded slowly. "How did they die?"

"Like most people. Defending what they had."

"But this place wasn't looted," he said.

"No it wasn't. My parents owned two stores in town. The café and a convenience store just off Depot Street. The place was ransacked, they were both shot in the head. The only consolation I have is they didn't suffer."

"I'm sorry," Damon said looking down into his drink before taking a swig. There was a minute or two of silence before she continued.

"So your friend here said you came back because…"

"Look, it's not easy out there. You know that." He gestured to Jesse. "We didn't know each other six months ago."

"I know, he told me."

Damon continued, "I just figured that maybe you…"

"You figured I couldn't exist without a little help?"

He shrugged. "Everyone needs a hand."

"Is that what you've told others you've met?"

"Yeah. I mean, no."

Her lip curled up. "It's okay, you don't need to explain."

Jesse leaned back in his chair. "By the way. Just out of curiosity. Did you plan to miss when you shot at him?" Jesse asked.

"Maybe. Maybe not."

Damon went to get up, and he groaned.

"You might want to sit there for a while before you try to move."

He scowled. "Did you really have to hit me so damn hard?"

"Like I said."

"Yeah, I got it," he replied. "So you've been surviving

here for two months?"

"About that. Things got really bad in Lake George. I had to get out, and I assumed my parents would still be alive but..." She trailed off again, her lip quivered. For someone who acted strong, she wasn't immune to the pain.

Damon leaned forward, clasping his hands together. "We don't have much but you are more than welcome to come with us."

"Any women?" she asked.

"Three. Well, four if you include Elliot's kid."

"Elliot?"

"One of the two we came here with."

She studied his face while nodding slowly. "If you're scavenging here, things can't be good in Lake Placid."

"No but we've planted seeds and we watch each other's backs."

She got up and walked over to the window and looked out. "I don't know." Ella placed a hand against the white frame.

Damon got up and squeezed the bridge of his brow. "Anyone else besides us attempted to enter?"

"A couple."

"And?"

"They're buried out back."

He took a deep breath. "I feel special," he said realizing how close they'd come to death. She let out a laugh before heading back in and picking up her cup of coffee.

"Things are only going to get worse."

"I already know that."

"So come with us."

He eyed Jesse across the room. His eyes darted between them.

Her fingers tapped out a beat against her leg. "I'll consider it."

"Of course," he said.

"It's just I feel safe here."

He nodded. "Right."

Jesse looked amused as he watched the back and forth between them.

"Well I guess I should grab a few belongings."

"So you've made up your mind?" Damon asked.

"Like I said, I'd consider it."

Confused, he shook his head as she turned away. "You need a hand?"

"Not unless you are good at picking out underwear."

Jesse snorted as she walked out back. He slapped him on the chest. "You're crazy." He headed over to the window and peered out and for a second he continued to smile. That quickly disappeared as he pulled back and pressed himself against the wall.

"Jesse?" Damon asked, his brow furrowing.

He raised four fingers, and Damon knew that meant trouble.

Chapter 4

By late afternoon the sun was beginning to wane behind the trees. Summer in Lake Placid was a hell of a lot more comfortable than the previous winter months. Temperatures were hovering in the high seventies, a stark difference to below freezing. When Elliot lost his house in the fire six months ago, Gary offered to have them stay at his home, but after everything they'd been through they opted to remain in the shelter. Although they were desperately short on food supplies, the bunker offered protection that none of the homes or buildings in the town could. Unlike others who were worried about home invaders, they slept well at night and only had to deal with threats by day.

Six months had changed everybody. It was surprising how quickly some people adapted while others buckled. Some held their ground while others fled. Rarely did a day go by when they didn't see smoke rising in the air or hear gunfire. The once pleasant town had morphed into streets full of violence. The EMP brought out the worst and best in people. Residents from ten homes along Mirror Lake Drive had banded together and created their own blockade on the north and south side of the road. There was little to worry about from the east, as there were several miles of thick woodland, and to the west, the lake.

Rayna had just returned from pulling a four-hour shift on the south end when she found Maggie in front of the ham radio. "CQ, CQ, CQ, calling CQ. This is WR7YZ." She glanced at her and smiled as she hung up the rifle and checked in with the kids who were in the back with Kong.

"This is New Hope Springs," a male voice replied.

"Can you provide your call sign?"

"SHN2UW."

"SHN2UW, this is WR7YZ calling out of Lake Placid. Where are you?"

"East Texas."

Over the course of the next few minutes Rayna listened to the conversation. Maggie had been spending a lot of time on the ham radio getting updates on FEMA camps as well as trying to find out if anyone from Kansas had survived. If the reports were anything to go by, the nukes had hit Kansas, California and West Virginia. The extent of the damage was still unknown, but it was safe to say that if her family were in Kansas at the time, they were probably dead. From what Elliot had learned from the news prior to the EMP, North Korea had conducted several nuclear weapon tests and the last one was more powerful than either of the bombs dropped by the U.S. in World War Two. In fact it was said they had one that tested at 120 kilotons. Compared to Little Boy or Fat Man, which was between 15 and 21 kilotons, that was powerful. On average it was estimated it would have inflicted more than 150,000 casualties, and that would have come from the initial blast radius. As for beyond that, well, it would have created less radioactive fallout compared to a surface blast which would have sucked up debris into the atmosphere, irradiated it and spread it for miles. Fortunately no matter what the fallout was, it was reduced rapidly in the first twenty-four hours. Again no one truly knew the extent of it but Elliot believed prevailing winds had assisted in pushing away much of the radioactive fallout, if there was much at all.

Maggie lowered the microphone and leaned back in her seat. "Did you catch all of that?" she asked without even looking at her.

"Some," Rayna replied, running a hand through Kong's hair.

Maggie turned her head. "There is a 650-acre complex with enough food to last the next three years for over 1,700 people. They currently have just over a hundred slots filled."

Rayna stroked the back of Kong's neck and nodded slowly. "That's good. It's going to help a lot of people."

"What about us?"

"What about us?" she said throwing the question back at her.

"We are scraping the bottom of the barrel here, Rayna. I've seen it. You've seen it. Hell, the rest of the families have. We need to start thinking long-term."

"We are. That's why they're out there right now."

She scoffed and shook her head. "And every day they come back with less. These small towns didn't have enough to begin with, and it's been six months."

"I know."

"So?"

Rayna frowned. "What do you want me to say, Maggie? What? You want to go to Texas? You know how far away that is?"

"I know it's far but—"

"No buts, look…" Rayna got up, went over to a shelf, pulled out a map and spread it over the table. She took out a red marker pen and circled Lake Placid. "By car we are looking at close to a two thousand mile journey. That's close to 30 hours without stopping. Now add to that the state of the roads, the unexpected attacks, and we could be looking at a week."

"But can't we at least see what it's about?"

Rayna shook her head and looked over at Lily and Evan who were reading magazines and drinking pop. She wanted the best for them, she really did, and if she was honest, she knew they were getting dangerously close to not being able to feed their own kids. It was one thing to go hunting when only a handful of hunters were doing it in season; it was another to know that thousands of people in upstate New York were doing the same. The deer population, which had once thrived, was dwindling. Most of the time when Gary and Elliot returned they brought back rabbit or squirrel. No one complained, but it was getting harder to find a good source of food. She'd planted all types of seeds from carrots, potatoes, beans, corn, cucumber, lettuce, onions, peas and so on and they'd reaped a good harvest but was it enough? Crops were becoming the new gold. Everyone wanted them and few had taken the initiative to gather seeds the way Elliot had before the EMP. Now they were sharing what they had with the other ten families as word soon spread and well, if they didn't share, their neighbors would have turned into adversaries and they had enough of those already.

Maggie continued, "The other families can go with us. That's more than enough protection. There are at least two people per household. Including us we are looking at twenty-five to thirty people being able to watch our backs as we make our way down."

"Not everyone has the means," Rayna replied. "Or the desire."

"This isn't about desire. It's about survival. You and Elliot of all people should know that."

"Look, Maggie, I get it but to reach Texas we have to go through the eye of the storm." She turned back to the map and drew a line from Lake Placid to Texas. It went between Kansas and West Virginia.

"But it was a high-altitude detonation. It's been six months."

"That doesn't mean it's not dangerous. We're safer here."

"For how long? And even if we are, how long realistically can we last? The winters are brutal up here. At least down there we stand a chance of being able to survive. Hell, it might even be better than the FEMA camp Gary was talking about."

She frowned. "Gary was speaking about going to a FEMA camp?"

Maggie shifted her weight from one foot to the next. "Yeah. You didn't know that?"

While her conversations with Jill had improved, things between them weren't the same. Jill harbored deep-seated resentment, and it didn't matter what Gary, Elliot or Rayna told her, it was clear the relationship would never mend. It was like a cut that had healed over. The scar still remained and every time they saw each other, they were reminded of what had caused it. Rayna brushed past Maggie on her way out to speak to Jill who was taking a shift at the north blockade.

"Where are you going?" Maggie asked.

"We'll talk later."

"But—"

"No. Later," she replied.

Rayna made her way past the charred remains of her home and turned up the street passing Bobby Wilmington and his wife, Susan. They gave a curt nod but said nothing. She'd come to know more about her neighbors in six months than she'd ever known before. It was amazing what stories people would share around the campfire at night. Everyone had a history, a reputation and opinions — not all of them jibed with hers but that was okay. Everyone was entitled to his or her view.

Jill was speaking to a group of three when she approached. She spotted her and Rayna raised two fingers to indicate she wanted to talk.

"Everything okay?" Jill asked. They were always concerned when Elliot and Gary went out. There was a chance they might not come back, but that was the cost of surviving. Danger lurked everywhere, and it didn't stop to ask if you had a family.

"Yeah, yeah, everything's good." She took a deep

breath. "I was meaning to talk to you about the FEMA camps. Is Gary serious about that?"

She pursed her lips and adjusted the rifle strap around her shoulder. No matter what background people had, even if they had never fired a gun before, within the first two months almost everyone was trained in how to hold, use, and clean a weapon. Although it was vital to learn some had refused. Jill wasn't one of them; she'd already been trained by Gary.

"Yeah. We've talked about heading south tomorrow or in a couple of days, to the FEMA camp just north of the Big Apple."

"And when were you going to bring this up?"

"Does it matter?" Jill asked.

"You know it matters. We rely on each other to get through each day."

"But aren't you tired of trying? I know I am."

Rayna stared back at her with a look of astonishment. At no point had they discussed this with Elliot or her.

"Do you really think it's going to be any better than

here, Jill?"

"It can't be any worse," she replied.

Rayna let out a heavy sigh and ran her fingers through her long dark hair. She looked over to Tristan Summers, Zach Matthews and Sean Young. They were oblivious to it all. Most of what they knew about the EMP and FEMA had come from what they'd shared so far. They were ordinary folk not given to disaster preparation.

"When Elliot returns we need to talk about this as a group."

"Rayna, as much as I appreciate your concern, this is something we're doing for us."

"Don't you mean you?" Rayna asked.

Jill folded her arms and narrowed her gaze. "No. It's for me and Gary."

Rayna shifted her weight. "And what about us?"

She shrugged. "You are more than welcome but I don't see Elliot wanting to do that."

"And that's why you're doing it. This isn't about survival, it's about you and me, isn't it?" Rayna asked.

"That's in the past."

"Is it? Because I still get the sense that you harbor resentment towards me."

"What do you want me to say, Rayna? I'm not going to stand here and lie to you and pretend it didn't happen."

"Elliot and Gary have managed to work things out."

"So?"

Rayna placed a hand on Jill's arm. "Can't we?"

Jill pulled away and breathed in deeply. "I don't hold any animosity towards you, Rayna. What we are planning is for us. We need this. I need this."

Rayna nodded. "So you're saying Elliot knows?"

"Gary was going to speak to him today about it." She looked over her shoulder. "Listen, I have to get back. We'll talk later."

Rayna agreed and walked away, her mind full of questions, concerns and worry. She knew entering a FEMA camp wasn't going to fly with Elliot but a camp run by ordinary people — maybe.

* * *

The first rule of engagement in order to survive against a threat was not to engage unless it was absolutely necessary. Stupid people ran into the heat of battle, allowing their egos to get the better of them. Smart individuals assessed, planned and then took action. Action didn't always mean going head to head. *Pick your battles,* Elliot had said. Damon and Jesse waited in silence as Ella returned. Jesse's heartbeat was slamming inside his chest and a bead of sweat rolled down his temple. A flashback from the beating he'd got made his stomach feel queasy. Panic was rising in his chest. He closed his eyes trying to calm his mind.

"Jesse. Jesse," Damon said. Jesse's eyelids popped open. "You good?"

He nodded, adjusting his grip on the Glock that he was holding with both hands down low. They'd heard the conversation below the window. The men were searching for Ella.

"I'm telling you, I saw her go around the back of these

buildings," a gruff voice said.

"Did you check inside?"

"By myself? No. She might not have been alone."

"What about that window up there?"

"It wasn't broken the last time I was here."

"Well get on up there. Go check it out."

Jesse heard the sound of a man jumping up a few times, reaching for the ladder and then yanking it down. They all heard the scraping of metal and boots pounding against steel while a man grumbled. "She's probably staying in that hotel four blocks down. No one is going to stay in an apartment with a broken window."

Damon gestured to Ella to head back while he chambered a round in his gun, raised it and prepared for the man to poke his head through the window. He slid against the wall to the right of the window while Jesse headed with Ella out the door and into the stairwell. Ella shrugged off Jesse's grip as he motioned for her to keep going. Damon wanted to tell her to stop being so stubborn but she wasn't having any of it. Instead she pulled the Sig Sauer from the front of her waistband and headed back in, sinking down behind the sofa, out of view but at the ready. Jesse shrugged and took cover behind a chair. Anyone looking in would see an empty room, unless of course they turned their head and then it would be a bullet.

Damon slowed his breathing in preparation as the sound of boots got louder, closer and… just as he saw the man's shadow against the floor inside, he heard the other man's voice.

"Ricky, get down here, we'll have to do it later. Seems we got company on the west side."

For a few breathless moments he listened to their verbal tennis until the man walked away from the window and descended. A minute or two later they heard them leave. Once they were gone he turned to Ella and said, "Still think you're safe?"

Chapter 5

Elliot arrived in Lake Placid shortly after nine that evening. The journey back had been filled with silence after a brief argument between Damon and Elliot concerning Ella. It wasn't that he didn't want to help her but they were already struggling to feed mouths. At some point a line in the sand had to be drawn. Damon refused to budge. A small group of neighbors came out to meet them, hoping to see what kind of haul they'd brought back. Expressions of hope soon vanished as they unloaded the Jeep.

"That's all?" Sean asked.

"Afraid so," Elliot replied.

"You look like you've been in a war," Tristan added.

Right then Jill made her way down and a look of horror spread across her face at the sight of Gary's bloody gash. The wound wasn't from the katana but from having slipped and knocked his head on the counter inside the store. Still, it was a nasty cut. One half of his face was caked in dry blood.

"What in heaven's name?"

"It's okay, Jill."

"It's not okay." She tossed Elliot a glare as if he was responsible for his safety. "Let me get that cleaned up. And we need to talk."

Four months ago, Gary and Jill moved into Mr. Thompson's house so they could be closer. They'd stayed in their home for a while until it got too dangerous. Besides, it made life easier to have them closer — that way everyone could share what they had and support each other. Elliot watched as the ten families hauled in the supplies. It would all be distributed out evenly between the families. Three months ago they were fending for themselves but the need to constantly hunt or scavenge meant taking everyone along or leaving them behind, and that was too risky. Gary was the one to come up with the plan. He'd handed out flyers to those on the street who were interested in combining resources in exchange for doing different tasks. Some would man the blockades while others searched for supplies. It was working but as the demand for food increased and supplies dwindled, it was getting harder to justify working together.

Elliot watched Damon lead Jesse and Ella off to the bunker. They passed Rayna on the way and she glanced at Ella before looking back at him.

Rayna's brow pinched. "Elliot, who's that?"

"Ask Damon. He's the one who found her and insisted that she come back."

"But you said we weren't going to be helping anyone else."

"And I meant it. Try telling that to him. That kid is on another wavelength."

She nodded. "So, how did you get on? Any food?"

"If you can call a few boxes of muffins food, yeah. I'm sure we can distribute out the chocolate chips and last a few more months," he said sarcastically.

She gripped him by the arm. "Well I'm glad you're back, we need to talk."

He sighed, reaching into his pocket for a cigarette. "Can't it wait until tomorrow? I'm exhausted. I can barely string together two thoughts."

"No. It will be too late by then."

"What is it?"

"Has Gary spoken to you about heading to a FEMA camp?"

He nodded.

"And?"

"It's just hot air. He won't leave."

"Not according to Jill. She sounded serious." She took a deep breath. "Anyway, there's another camp. Maggie connected with a group down in East Texas called New Hope Springs. Apparently they have more than enough food to last for the next three years for 1,700 people. They have less than a hundred there right now."

"That's a lot of food."

"It's a lot of people."

He studied her face. "Hold on a minute. Why do I get a sense you are suggesting we head down there?"

"I'm not. I'm just saying it's an alternative that we should discuss in light of the fact that Gary and Jill are heading out tomorrow."

"Whoa! Tomorrow? He never said anything about that."

"Well, she did. They're leaving tomorrow morning, Elliot, for a FEMA camp near the Big Apple."

"That's insane."

"My thoughts exactly."

He shifted his weight from one foot to the next and squinted. "Are you considering it?"

"I'm..." she trailed off and sighed. "My home is with you. Where you go, I go, but we have Lily and Evan to think about. I won't let them starve, Elliot."

"And you think the solution is to hand over our weapons and walk into a FEMA camp?"

"I didn't say that," she said. "I'm suggesting that we discuss New Hope Springs. If it has enough to feed 1,700 for the next three years, we need to jump on that now before others join them. It's going to fill up fast."

Elliot shook his head. "No, something doesn't sound right. Why would anyone open their doors to strangers?"

"We did."

"For three people." He looked off toward the bunker as Ella climbed down. "Okay, four people but that's a big difference compared to 1,700."

"Is it?"

Elliot scoffed. "You have spent too much time around Jill and Gary. They've infected your mind with the... society is going to go back to normal."

"Don't belittle me, Elliot, or put words in my mouth. I'm just saying that not all of society is going to push people out. Look at what we've been able to accomplish with just ten families. Now imagine 1,700 people working together. Who knows how quickly life could change for the better?"

"Or the worst."

"Why are you so damn negative all the time?"

"Negative? I'm a realist! Think about it, Rayna, society has collapsed. There are thousands upon thousands of people in towns and cities all over the country that are in dire straits. Now, ask yourself this… why would anyone open their doors and allow their supplies to dwindle?"

"Why did we? We could have ignored our neighbors, but we didn't."

"No, but there was a reason why. We…" He started to become at a loss for words. She was good at communicating, whereas he was just a mess, especially when he was hungry and tired, and damn he was hungry. "We needed help."

"And maybe they're the same."

Elliot scoffed. "You're jumping the gun, Rayna. Besides, it's a long way to Texas and what happens if we're wrong? Huh? What happens if it's a bad situation? I'm not going to place your life or the kids' in danger. At least here we can cope. We know how it works here."

She pointed to the town as smoke spiraled up. "There have been more fires started, more homes burned to the ground. Things are out of control. It's only a matter of time before raiders show up here on this street. We are not prepared for them. Besides, people are hungry. We've bled this county dry. You've been out there and every time you come back with fewer supplies. Unless you can think of something better, this might be our only hope."

Elliot exhaled hard and leaned against the Jeep and took a drag on his cigarette. Kong came bounding over with Lily and Evan. Both of them wrapped their arms around him and he smiled. He nodded. "Okay, let's talk about it. Get Gary and Jill together. We'll take a vote on it."

Rayna leaned in and kissed him on the lips.

Just as he went to tell the kids to head over to Gary's place with Rayna, an epic explosion shattered the silence. Fire licked up into the night sky from one of the homes farther down the street.

"That's my place!" Tristan Summers yelled, making a mad dash.

The rest of them followed but not before Elliot told the kids to get down in the bunker. He scooped up his AR-15 and double-timed it after the rest of the group. As they got closer two individuals emerged from the home, fleeing on foot with armfuls of supplies. Sean and Zach gave chase but it was pointless. They hopped into a white truck and tore away. It was the same one that had been stolen from the police department a few months back.

"My kids are inside," Tristan yelled as she tried to make her way in. Rayna physically restrained her as Elliot dashed into the smoke-filled building calling out her kids' names.

"Jana. Kendrick."

He could hear crying. As he pushed in, a large chunk of ceiling collapsed cutting off the way. He coughed and gagged, covered his mouth and nose with his arm as he squinted into the darkness and flames.

"Here!" Damon appeared behind him with a blanket soaked in water. He placed it over him and pulled him out. They circled around the house looking for another way in. Elliot used the back of his rifle to smash the rear windows on the house.

"Elliot. No. It's too dangerous."

He ignored him and climbed inside and continued calling out their names. The smoke was even more intense. They must have used some type of accelerant because there was no other way it could have burned this fast. He struggled to breathe as he moved through into the hallway trying to reach the stairs. Damon was close behind as he hopped over burning debris and ascended the staircase that was now engulfed in flames. If it weren't for the soaking wet blanket, he wouldn't have been able to get that far inside. He could feel the heat from beneath it as he pressed on shouting out their names. When he reached the second floor, he followed the sound of crying and entered a room to find a young black girl cowering in the corner holding her teddy. He scooped her up and shouted for Damon to check the next room but the fire was too intense. He backed up as Elliot handed Jana to him. "Get her out of here."

"Elliot, it's going to collapse. We need to go now."

"Just get her out!"

He didn't hesitate and scooped up Jana, covering her

in his blanket and then disappearing into the black smoke. Elliot coughed hard and navigated his way around flaming debris. Chunks of ceiling were engulfed and fumes coming off plastic were making it hard to breathe. He called out to the older kid but didn't get any response. He checked two more rooms but couldn't see shit because there was so much smoke. As he turned to head out, the ceiling collapsed cutting off his way. He hurried back into the room he was coming out of and approached the glass and pushed the window open. The sudden intake of air caused a backdraft. A whooshing sound and flames came at him; he covered his face with the blanket but could feel the searing heat as it bore down on him. He gasped for air and crawled out of the window, rolling down a portion of the lower roof before dropping to the yard below. When he landed someone rushed over with a bucket of water and tossed the contents all over him to put out the flames. Once they were extinguished, he threw the blanket off. From across the yard, coughing and spluttering, Tristan cried out hysterically. "Where is he? Where is my boy?"

Elliot couldn't answer her without coughing. Her son was gone. There wasn't enough time to get them both. Her knees buckled, and she fell to the ground sobbing while holding her sole surviving child. Rayna rushed to help Elliot, placing her arms around him.

"I'm sorry," Elliot muttered. "I tried."

His words were lost in her cries.

The flames engulfed the clapboard home and within minutes the place was a roaring inferno. Elliot looked at his wife and she didn't need to say it, he knew what she was thinking. This was the beginning of the end for them.

* * *

An hour later, those that would or could attend gathered around a campfire in Elliot's backyard. It was a somber atmosphere. Tristan wasn't there, Susan Wilmington was taking care of her. The conversation that night revolved around the obvious need to leave Lake Placid.

"I don't have to explain. It's pretty obvious. We stay, we starve or die," Gary said. "Now Jill and I are planning on leaving tomorrow for a FEMA camp on the outskirts of New York City. Now you are all welcome to come... or stay."

"There is one other option," Maggie said, interrupting. She brought everyone up to speed on what she'd heard over the radio earlier that evening.

"I'm not sure if it's real or just a ploy to trap people but not everyone is onboard with going to a FEMA camp," Rayna said, walking around the campfire as everyone looked on. Shadows danced on their faces from the fire, a look of stress, strain and sadness dominated. "We feel we should take a vote. Those of you in favor of leaving put up your hands."

In attendance that night there were eight of the ten families. Everyone had been informed that it was going to be a discussion about leaving Lake Placid and not everyone wanted to leave. The town was their home no matter how bad things got. The dangers beyond were self-explanatory. Eighteen people put up their hands to leave.

"I'm all for leaving but I'm thinking that FEMA

sounds better than this New Hope Springs. First off it's too far away. Second, we would have to go directly past Kansas and West Virginia and who knows what the danger level of radiation is like there. Sure, we are fine here and it's been six months but we are taking a huge risk heading down there. Why don't we all head for FEMA?" Bobby Wilmington asked.

"We can," Elliot added. "But are you willing to hand over your weapons?"

"I never carried before. So it's no skin off my nose," he replied.

"I'm not handing mine over," Zach said in a defiant tone.

"Then the decision is made," Gary said. "Those who are okay with laying down your weapons, you'll go to FEMA with us. Those who aren't can go with Elliot."

Elliot stared at his old friend across the campfire. Everyone was seated on logs. Jill stood behind Gary rubbing the back of his neck. Elliot got up and motioned to Gary to have a word with him.

"No, anything you want to say you can say in front of all of us," he said.

"Okay," Elliot said. "Why?"

"Why what?"

"Why divide now? You were all for sticking together when the shit hit the fan. And now it's out of control, you want to divide us up?"

"I don't want to divide anyone. We're just making a different decision."

"Which in turn is dividing us. We are stronger together."

Gary rose to his feet. "Then come with us to the FEMA camp."

"It's not happening."

"Then who's the one dividing?" Gary replied.

With that said he turned to the others. "I'll be leaving at seven in the morning. Anyone who wants to come with me is welcome. To the rest of you, good luck." Jill wrapped her arm around his waist and they walked away without even giving them another look.

Chapter 6

In the early hours of the morning Ryan Hayes crept out of his quarters with one thing in mind — killing military members. He was going against everything that Harlan had instructed them to do in the event the compound was taken but if he didn't take action, who would? Of course he didn't plan on killing them all, just a few, enough to give them second thoughts about staying.

He'd spent eight years in the U.S. Army and two years with the Dallas Police Department before the EMP. In many ways his life was damn near perfect. A great woman, zero kids, two vacations a year and the admiration of those he knew. All of that changed when the lights went out.

He'd spent the first week assisting the department as they tried to stop looters and gangs from taking the law into their own hands. It turned out to be an utter failure. Without a means of getting around the city, violence soon spiraled out of control and he knew if he didn't get out he would probably die at the hands of an angry mob.

Fortunately, their father had purchased one of the bunkers two years prior after getting worried about the state of the country. He'd sunk his entire retirement savings into the property with the firm belief that one day they would need it.

He was right.

It was a risky investment but it paid off.

Now to have someone come in and try to take that away wasn't just an insult, it was disrespectful to his father's wishes. At least FEMA reps who had shown up two weeks after the collapse had the good sense to approach the gate and inquire about using the property without showing force.

Not these fools.

They could say whatever they liked about being pro-American and against the government but at the end of the day they were the ones treating them like prisoners. They were nothing more than cold-blooded killers, no better than looters in the city. This wasn't about survival, it was control, and as long as they were at the helm life wouldn't get any better.

Under the cover of darkness, Ryan carried a serrated hunting knife and peered around one of the buildings in the village. His target was a single military member who was positioned two blocks down. The beauty of the property was its size; they couldn't watch over the residents and patrol the area without leaving some areas exposed. He intended to take full advantage of that.

Dressed in full black, a hoodie up and his face darkened out with camo face paint, he moved quickly, closing the distance between him and the soldier. He understood the dangers, but they'd already taken his father's life. Now it was time for some retribution.

His movements were smooth and purposeful. Ryan darted in and out of the shadows, keeping his back to the wall until he was within thirty feet of his target. He crouched down and waited for him to walk back to the corner of the building. He'd had him under surveillance for the past ten minutes, observing where he moved. The key to this was surprise. The soldier's finger was near the trigger. If Ryan didn't act fast, and the soldier managed to squeeze off a round, not only would he wind up injured but it would also sound the alarm and that was the last thing he needed.

He listened to the soldier's boots get closer. Ryan tightened his grip on the leather handle and ran through exactly what he was about to do. His heart started racing. The anticipation made sweat form on his brow. He didn't enjoy killing but after what they'd done, he wouldn't think twice or lose sleep.

The soldier strolled by and made a turn. As he did, Ryan jumped and jabbed the knife into the side of his neck with one hand and knocked the gun away from his finger with his other arm. The soldier slumped, and he dragged him to the ground, pulling his body into the shadows. He relieved him of the M4 and a Glock, as well as additional magazines, and then removed his radio.

He didn't linger.

A quick check to make sure no one had seen him. He listened to the radio and heard a couple of soldiers talking shit about women in the compound. Good. He was in the clear. Ryan hurried back to his point of entry and made his way down the steel ladder into the tunnels. It was dark inside. He knew where the cameras were and made sure to avoid them as he hurried through the underground network that linked up each of the bunkers. This time he headed for the chapel at the south end. He had one more kill in mind before the sun came up.

* * *

Elliot didn't sleep much that night. Since his return to Lake Placid his mind had been preoccupied with staying alive. He wasn't anticipating leaving. *That wasn't in the plans,* he thought. He also didn't expect to become so attached to those around him.

He looked at Rayna who was still sleeping. Her chest rose and her lips moved ever so slightly. God, he would do anything for her. At the foot of their bed on two air mattresses were his kids. Kong raised an eyebrow as Elliot got up and slipped into some clothes. He glanced at his watch. It was just after five-thirty. His stomach was grumbling, and he needed to take a piss. He slipped into his boots and Kong got up to go with him.

"No, you stay here. I can't haul you up."

His head cocked.

"It's okay, I'm not going anywhere."

He'd often wondered if the dog knew what he was feeling — the anxiety, the sense of impending doom that hung heavy every day. He didn't like living that way, but that was life now. He yawned, rubbed at his eyes and headed out the rear escape hatch so that he didn't wake Damon and the others who were sleeping farther down in the bunker.

Once he was topside, he relieved himself in the bushes before reaching into his pocket for a pack of smokes. *Shit!* He crumpled the empty packet.

"Need a smoke?" Gary said. Elliot twisted to find him ambling through the forest. He nodded and once he made his way over he took one.

"Won't be long and we'll have no choice but to quit."

"I guess," Elliot replied lighting his. "You didn't sleep last night?"

"Not much," Gary replied, looking off into the distance.

Elliot blew smoke out his nostrils. "Look, about last night."

Gary screwed up his face. "Let's not talk about it."

"No, we need to. I understand why you're heading to FEMA. I get it. It's just that we've been through a lot over the past six months. I thought if we stuck together—"

"Enough, Elliot. It's too damn early in the morning and I haven't even had any coffee."

He walked out of the woods into the clearing of Elliot's backyard and over to the campfire where there was a blackened pot. "You got some coffee?" he asked.

"Down in the bunker."

Elliot watched him disappear inside. He took a few more logs and threw them on the fire and took a seat. He cast his eyes over the remains of his home. It was hard to believe it was gone. While he was lost in thought, Gary returned and put some water on to boil. He took a seat beside him.

"How are you going to get down to the city?" Elliot asked.

"The Jeep."

"We're taking that."

"So you're onboard with heading to Texas?"

"I am now."

He scoffed. "You're only saying that because you want to make it hard for us."

"The Jeep was ours to begin with," Elliot replied.

"But it became property of the department."

"And where are they now?"

There was silence between them. Obtaining transportation had become tough. Raiders had stolen one of their trucks in the night, and another one was taken by force months ago. Gary went over to the pot and poured out two cups of coffee. He handed one off to Elliot and returned to his seat. He gave it a stir while staring into the fire. It popped and crackled, an orange glow warmed their faces.

Gary sniffed his mug. "Ah that first drop of coffee in the morning."

"Doesn't get any better."

Both of them chuckled.

"Listen, Gary, how about you come with us, check out this compound? If it's not good, we'll head to the FEMA camp."

"You'll enter?" he asked.

"I didn't say that. But I'll personally drop you off." Elliot smiled.

"Right, and let me be the guinea pig."

"Hey, it was your idea."

They continued drinking coffee and smoking as the sun started to come up, its deep orange light filtered through the dense pines.

Elliot raised his arms and stretched. "Anyway, I don't think we're going to have enough space in the Jeep for everyone. Some of us are going to need horses."

"And where do you plan on finding those? Anything that has four legs has become food, barring Kong," Gary said with a smile.

"Yeah, don't let him hear that." Elliot chuckled. "Lake Placid Horseback Riding. It's a twenty-minute drive outside of town. I took Lily and Evan there a few years back. It's a ranch just off County Route 18."

Gary frowned. "Okay, wait a second. You're telling me you knew about this place all this time?"

"Yeah," Elliot replied as if it wasn't a big thing.

"And you didn't think to tell us?"

"Well we had a Jeep."

"But there were some of us that could have used those horses."

"For food?"

"Damn right."

"That's why."

He frowned. "You've got to be joking. You mean you would rather starve than kill a horse?"

"Up until now there has been plenty of deer in the

wilderness for us to eat."

"But still we could have used the horses for transportation."

Elliot smirked. "Listen, even if I told you, how would you have kept those horses alive? We had enough on our plate as it was without the burden of having to feed ten horses. I figured the owners of the ranch would take care of them and when things got desperate, we'd head that way."

"Desperate?"

"Yep."

Gary ran a hand over his face. "How the hell did we end up here?"

"I've asked myself that countless times. People are people. Instead of seeing the good in each other, we keep picking out the faults to make up for our own inadequacies."

Gary drained the rest of his coffee, tossing the dregs into the fire before rising.

"Well let's go see what that ranch has to offer."

"But I thought you were leaving at seven."

"And I thought you were going to let us use the Jeep."

They both smiled at one another.

* * *

At just after seven, Ryan awoke to the sound of gunfire. A flood of memories came back from that morning's attack. He was surprised at how easy killing them had been. Of course he knew there would be consequences. He glanced at his hands one last time to make sure all the blood was gone. Even though he'd worn gloves, paranoia had kicked in. If there was even a drop of blood on him they'd probably find it. He'd removed his clothes, bagged them and hid them behind a ceiling tile. Outside his room he could hear shouting. Soldiers beat on doors for people to get up and head out.

A soldier burst into his room with an M4 pointed at his face.

"You! Let's go! Outside!"

He hurried past him, scooping up his boots on the way out. Their large group traversed the tunnels like ants until they emerged into the bright morning. Ryan squinted and brought an arm to his face to block the glare of the sun. One by one they were dragged, pushed and made to get on their knees in a straight line. The general emerged shoving his way through the crowd with his Glock by his side.

"I thought I had made myself clear about how this was going to work. Well it appears one or maybe some of you didn't understand. Two of my men are dead." He paced up and down staring intently at each of them. "Now I could go ahead and shoot two of you and that would send a clear message but I have a feeling you would just continue, and that would be too easy. The rest of you wouldn't suffer and for this… believe me, you're going to suffer." He stopped in front of Ryan but didn't look down, instead his eyes swept over everyone. "So, I'm going to give you until the count of twenty for someone to tell me who was responsible."

Ryan had made a point not to tell anyone. He knew there was a chance they would buckle under the pressure.

"Come on. If you don't tell me I'm going to cut your rations in half. That's right, you will work more, and get less food."

Harlan spoke up. "Perhaps it wasn't any of us. Have you thought about that? You blew two holes in the wall. Anyone could have got in last night."

Shelby eyed him with a look of death. "You're right. Someone could have." He turned and looked at his men and a smirk formed. "Guys, were you asleep at the walls last night?"

They shook their heads. "No."

"Did you see anyone enter?"

"Nope."

He turned back to Harlan. "So that rules that out. Now back to your group." He crouched down beside Harlan and grabbed a firm grip on his collar before dragging him out and shoving him in front of them all. "Which one of you was responsible? I want an answer and I want it now!"

Ryan glanced at Harlan but refused to say anything.

He was willing to eat less if it meant he could continue to kill. At the end of the day, the way he saw it — they needed them. They hadn't just broken through those walls so they could make use of the bunkers and food supply; they wanted more people working with them. That's what it was all about now. That was why this place had been created. He knew that. They knew that.

Shelby crouched beside Harlan and placed the Glock against his head.

"Do I really need to start executing people to get my point across? Cause I really don't want to have to do that."

A few cries were heard, but no one stepped forward to say they were the one. The general released his grip and paced for a few more minutes. "Okay. Do it your way. Today all of you are going to work on the walls to close the holes. You will work until they are complete. No food today. Do you hear me? You're getting no food! And for the one who did this — when I find you and I will, your death won't be fast."

Chapter 7

It should have taken exactly thirty minutes to reach County Road 18, however, it meant passing through Saranac Lake, a town that had nearly killed them the day before. Jesse didn't like the idea so he'd opted to hang back and help out with one of the blockades. With so much on the line and a need for people to ride back on horses, if there were any, they took as many people as they could fit into the Jeep with several others riding in the back of a trailer. Gary figured they'd only need five or six horses. One horse for two people would suffice.

They were heading north on NY-86, and were only minutes outside of Saranac Lake when Elliot saw the blockade in the distance.

"That wasn't there yesterday."

Elliot brought the Jeep to the shoulder of the road so he could get a better look with the binoculars.

"How many?" Gary asked.

"Three. All armed."

"You can head back and take 33 in," Ella said.

"If it's not blocked," Gary replied.

"It's the only other way you are getting through the town."

"What do you want to do?" Elliot asked Gary.

"What are you asking me?"

"Because you're the one that needs the horses."

He shook his head. "Just go around."

Elliot did a U-turn in the road and traveled roughly five minutes down the road to County Highway 33. It was a narrow, winding road referred to as McKenzie Pond Road. As it got closer to the town, it fed into Pine Street. Ella kept yakking on about it as if none of them was aware. "I told you," Ella said. "It's smooth sailing from here on out. Just follow this over to Bloomingdale Avenue and then hang a right on Broadway and take a left on Ampersand Avenue. That will take us onto County Route 18 and hopefully get us past any other blockade that's in place. I'm guessing they have one at the corner of

Edgewood and State Route 3, and maybe one on the north side."

Elliot scanned the homes as they passed them, weaving his way around stalled vehicles. "You say this as if you already knew about the blockades."

"They're not new. When you arrived yesterday, they had everyone searching for me." She said it without batting an eye. She stared out the window acting as if that remark wasn't going to raise further questions.

"Hold on a second, they were searching for you? Why?" Gary asked.

"I killed four of their men over the past two months, stole supplies and have basically been a thorn in their side since day one."

Gary turned in his seat. Even Damon was looking at her with wide eyes.

"You want to run that by me again?" Gary said.

"When I arrived here from Lake George there were no blockades. After I found my family dead, I tried to track down who'd killed them. Wasn't easy but just like Lake

Placid has its gangs, so does Saranac. I managed to lure a guy into a store and…"

"Lure?"

"Use your imagination, Damon," Gary said. "Continue."

"Anyway, before I killed him I got him to tell me how many other groups were operating in the town."

"And?"

"He said he only knew of two. Some idiot by the name of Dallas ran his group. He also admitted that his group was responsible for my parents' death, and most of those in town."

"And the other?"

"No longer in operation. Dallas forced them to get onboard with what he was doing or die."

Damon nodded. "So that's why those men were out searching for you."

"Bingo!" she said with a smirk on her face.

"Great, Damon brought back a psychopath," Gary muttered.

"Hey, I haven't done anything you all haven't done. So cut me some slack. Besides, those assholes killed my parents."

"Okay, okay," Gary said turning back in his seat. "But this is information I would have liked to have known before we headed out. If I'd known I would have left you at home. Now we have to hope we don't get..."

Before he could spit the words out, Elliot slammed on the brakes. They were like rats streaming out of the woodwork. One second the street was clear, nothing but abandoned vehicles, and the next, armed individuals rushed the vehicle. Knowing he had only seconds he switched on the radio and pressed the button.

"Come in, Maggie, this is Elliot. We're under attack. Saranac Lake. I repeat, Saranac Lake."

There had to have been fifteen. They swarmed the truck shouting for them to toss the keys out while raking their assault rifles.

"Well that explains why there was no blockade along this street," Gary said. Elliot looked in his rearview mirror at Sean, Zach and Bobby who were now surrounded. A man wearing camouflage gear, with sunken eyes and hair pulled back into a ponytail, came up to the driver's side window and tapped it. He had a cigarette in his mouth and an AR-15 hanging low. Elliot brought the window down.

"Get out."

His directions were straight to the point. No theatrics.

"Look, we don't mean any trouble," he replied.

Without saying another word, the man twisted around and fired a round into Bobby's head. His body slumped over the edge of the trailer to the ground.

"If I have to ask again, you're next."

Elliot turned off the engine and handed over the keys and slipped out. All of them were quickly disarmed, zip tied and had rope strung between them to keep them together. The group of men and women led them away while two of them hopped into their vehicle and drove off.

"Fucking great!" Elliot said.

"Well, had you told us about the horses before, maybe we wouldn't have needed to come here today," Gary muttered under his breath.

"Shut the hell up!" the grizzled-looking man said smacking Gary in the back of the shoulders with the butt of his rifle. Gary stumbled forward nearly losing his footing.

* * *

Maggie had been sitting by the ham radio running several questions by the owners of New Hope Springs when she heard Elliot come over the walkie-talkie beside her. She picked it up and replied but got no answer. Hurrying to the surface of the bunker she scanned the road for Rayna but she couldn't see her. Farther down the road Jesse was standing beside two neighbors when she came sprinting up, out of breath.

"It's Elliot. They're in trouble."

"What?"

She brought him up to speed. At first Jesse paced back and forth running a hand over his head. "Shit. What do we do?"

"We need to find Rayna, where is she?"

"She went into town with Jill."

"Do we have another vehicle?" Maggie asked.

"No."

Dismay swelled in her chest. This was the first time they hadn't had the input of Damon, Gary, Rayna or Elliot. They'd always turned to them for guidance.

"What about that vehicle that was stolen from the police?"

Jesse shook his head. "We don't have it. It could be anywhere."

"We've seen it six times over the past two weeks. It has to be with someone in this town."

"Well we don't have time to go searching."

A sense of despair washed over them as they waited for Rayna to return. In the meantime all they could do was hope that Elliot and the others would manage to get out of whatever predicament they were in.

* * *

It felt like they'd been walking for half an hour before they arrived at a bar called the Rusty Nail just off Broadway Street. It was a run-down joint made from faded brick and pine. All six of them were shoved through the dilapidated double doors. The aroma of alcohol attacked their senses as they were guided to a bar on the right where two men were chatting and drinking beers. Off to the left another four men played pool. A generator could be heard churning away. They were using it to provide light in the dingy interior.

"Dallas, we got them."

"Well done, guys." An ordinary-looking man turned on his seat. He wore a baseball cap, a crisp blue shirt, a pair of blue denim jeans and a sleeveless leather jacket where a patch had once been. He was average in size, close to six foot, and had to be in his early forties.

As he turned, he wagged his finger at Ella and smiled. He didn't get off the stool but instead just stared, looking her up and down like a piece of meat.

"Isn't this ironic? You've managed to elude me for

close to two months, had plenty of opportunities to run, and when I finally nab you, you're trying to get into Saranac." He slapped the heavily bearded guy beside him and laughed. He slipped off the stool and walked over and with a simple gesture of the eyes, and a slight nod, all of them were forced down to their knees. He reached down and ran a hand around Ella's face. "You and I have unfinished business. But right now I'm curious. Who are your friends? The last time I saw you, you were alone."

His eyes washed over them.

"No one, just people who gave me a ride."

"Really? How generous." He sniffed hard. "You wouldn't be lying to me?" he asked, walking over to her again and grabbing her chin and squeezing it with one hand.

"Get your hands off her!" Damon said. Elliot squeezed his eyes tight wishing he hadn't said anything. That was just asking for trouble.

"Oh, a hometown hero. And who might you be?"

"Someone who's seen people like you before."

"Is that so? And what type of people would that be?"

"Assholes with small dicks and big egos."

Dallas smiled and took another sip of his beer before he crouched down in front of Damon. "I've got to ask myself. What kind of man insults another when he's on his knees, zip tied and unarmed?" He paused for a second. "Don't answer that. Let me answer it for you." He rose and took off his jacket and flipped it around. "You see this?" He pointed to the outline of a patch. "This belonged to the leader of a motorcycle gang who thought they were going to take over Saranac. Of course they didn't have any bikes but they had balls, just like you. In fact, if I recall, he said something very similar to me right before I blew a hole in his skull." Dallas tossed the jacket onto the bar and pulled out a Smith & Wesson revolver from the back of his waistband. He pressed it against Damon's head.

"Now give me one good reason why you shouldn't join him in the shallow grave out back."

Elliot leaned forward on his knees. "Hey, c'mon, he

was just being an asshole," Elliot said coming to his defense. "He's always like that."

Dallas eyed him and repositioned a toothpick that was at the corner of his mouth. "You in charge?"

"No."

"I said are you in charge?"

"No."

"Then shut the fuck up!"

He turned back to Damon and looked as if he was contemplating killing him. He cocked the gun and Damon didn't even flinch. It wasn't hard to tell if he was ready to die. His actions were clear enough. Death was no longer something to be feared, in many ways it was a sweet relief from the hellish existence.

Dallas de-cocked the gun and slid it back into his jeans. He took another swig of his beer then offered Damon a drink. When Damon said nothing, Dallas turned it and poured the remainder over his head — golden liquid streamed down Damon's skin, dripping to the ground.

"There we go. Don't say I don't share."

He turned back to the bar and tossed the bottle behind it. From Elliot's position on the floor he could see hundreds of empty bottles scattered on the floor. "So, which one of you brave folks is going to tell me who you are, where you're from, where you were heading and what you are doing in my town? You see because I'm not sure how it works where you come from but here, things have changed." He went around the bar and pulled out a bottle of whiskey, unscrewed it and poured out three fingers into a glass. He tucked it back under and took a drink. "For instance, that road you just used has a toll on it. And what that means is if you use it, you are going to have to pay. Now, being as you have been good enough to hand over a set of wheels without incident, I'm going to take that as payment. And because you've given me this lovely gal," he said as he walked over and ran his hand around the back of Ella's head, "I'm going to be extremely lenient. In fact that's why your friend doesn't have a bullet in his skull right now." He glanced at Elliot. "Oh, did you think it was because you spoke on your friend's behalf?" He shook his head. "No. He's alive because you've given me two things I want. Now all I want is a few answers to my questions and then you can go on your way." He turned to his bearded friend at the bar. "That would be a first, wouldn't it, Vern?"

"That it would," he replied.

"So?"

Sean piped up before Elliot could speak. "Lake Placid. We were on our way to a ranch out on County Road 18. There are supposed to be horses there."

"Really?" He leaned against the bar taking a sip and smiling. "Oh this day is getting better by the minute. In fact, I'm starting to like this group. You know what, Vern, I might even offer them a drink."

"I wouldn't go that far," Vern replied.

He cocked his head. "Ah, maybe you're right." He gazed at them. "And what were you planning on doing with these horses?"

"Leaving Lake Placid and heading down to a FEMA

camp in New York, well, that's what Gary here wanted to do. Elliot wants to head to a compound in Texas."

"Oh, a divided house. Isn't that interesting?" He eyed them as if contemplating what to say next. Dallas took the bottle of whiskey off the counter and filled his glass again before taking a seat on a stool.

"And how many more of you are in Lake Placid?"

"Around ten families."

"Shut up," Elliot said to Sean. Dallas picked up on it.

"Oh don't worry, we don't have any reason to head your way. However, I am interested in that ranch. Those horses would come in real handy right about now. You see, I don't know about you but meat is hard to come by and I'm thinking a nice bit of rump horse would go down like a treat, what do you say, Vern?"

"Sounds good."

"Well then it looks like we have a road trip ahead of us."

Chapter 8

Across the country in East Texas, Ryan Hayes joined the rest of New Hope Springs in reconstructing the wall that those bastards had blown up. A hard morning sun bore down making them curse. There wasn't even a breeze. His brother Samuel Hayes grumbled as he mixed the concrete powder together while Ryan scooped it up into a wheelbarrow. Sweat dripped off his brow. They'd been at this for close to an hour and even with the hundred plus residents it wasn't easy.

Samuel was thirty-one, two years younger than Ryan — a fair-haired kid, strong, close to six foot. He'd been working as a paramedic before the lights went out. Both had grown up in a military family. Their father had been hard on them as he tried to instill the desire to serve their country like his father and his before. It worked. Both were in the military before pursuing other ways to serve their country.

"If dad was here, he wouldn't have let them get away with this."

"Well, he isn't, so it's down to us," Ryan replied.

"Those bastards didn't even allow us to give them a proper funeral."

After the attack on the compound, all those that had fallen were dragged away and piled up for a mass burial on the east side. They were treated no different than Jews by the Nazis — simply dumped into an unmarked grave without any regard for who they were or those left behind. When they would be buried was anyone's guess. It would have to be soon before they started to stink. No doubt it would be them who would have to do it.

"Whoever killed those men last night did us a favor. I hope they get more."

Ryan glanced at him but didn't say anything. He could have told him but that meant placing his life in jeopardy. If things went to plan that night he would kill another two. After that, there was no telling if Shelby would interrogate and if he did, what methods he'd use. A part of him knew the risk but what other option did he have? He was only able to pull it off because he'd seen the blueprint of the underground tunnels and knew where the air ducts led. That was how he'd managed to get out of his room without being seen.

"Maybe they will," he replied. Samuel gave him a questioning look. He glanced around a few times and then came over and grabbed him.

"That better not have been you."

Ryan pushed him back. "And if it was?"

"It's one thing to kill them, another to put your life in danger. I've already lost dad, I'm not losing you."

"And you won't."

Ryan eyed the armed soldiers walking back and forth like prison guards making sure the chain gang wasn't slacking. If they didn't maintain a good pace, they would come up and shove them with the butt of their rifles. His eyes roamed to where Shelby was sitting, drinking beer and observing them like an Egyptian pharaoh. Their eyes locked and Ryan looked away. He picked up a wheelbarrow and pushed it over to the wall. After dropping it, he sat down to catch his breath when a soldier approached him.

"You. Come with me."

Ryan wiped sweat from his brow and followed him, passing by Samuel who eyed him while continuing to work. The soldier led him to the stands, which were in front of the archery field. The soldier told him where to stop and wait. Shelby took another swig of his drink before speaking. "Harlan says you were involved with the tactical division, is that right?"

He nodded without giving a verbal response.

"What's your name?"

"Ryan Hayes."

"How long were you in the military?"

"Long enough."

Shelby smirked.

"You wouldn't by any chance know who was behind the deaths of my two men last night, would you?"

He didn't hesitate in shaking his head. Shelby wiped

his lips with a napkin after finishing off a plate of food before stepping down from the stands and walking over.

"Did you train these people to fight?"

"Tried to."

"I like that. Tried. It allows room for error. No one is held responsible if you… tried." He smiled and blew cigarette smoke in his face. "You want one?"

Ryan nodded. He might have turned him down but part of the reason he was on edge was a lack of nicotine. Since they'd arrived he hadn't had one. He looked over his shoulder towards the others. Shelby continued, "Go on. I can see you want one. Don't worry about what they think."

He took it and placed it between his lips and Shelby lit it. He breathed in deeply and for a few seconds felt at ease before Shelby placed his arm around him and led him over to the bench.

"Take a load off your feet. Have a beer."

Ryan reached into a bucket and pulled one out. It was warm.

"I kind of miss ice, don't you?" Shelby asked.

Ryan shrugged, cracked it open and downed it because they'd skimped on giving them water.

"You know all of this would have happened, anyway. I mean, repairing the wall. It's just a pity you have to suffer through it. Now if I knew who was responsible. Maybe I could reduce that suffering."

He paused, waiting for Ryan to respond.

Shelby stuck his tongue in his cheek and leaned forward holding a cigarette in one hand and a beer in the other. "Look, I'll get straight to the point. I really don't want to have to kill any more people. That's not what I had in mind when we arrived, despite what you might think. No, the only way this engine will run smoothly is with all of us working together. And I'll be the first to admit, it's going to take some work for you all to trust me but that's where I thought you might come in. Harlan says these folks look up to you."

"He'd be mistaken. I'm not in charge," Ryan replied.

"No, but you were the first to step outside the

bunker."

Ryan frowned. "And?"

"It means you were willing to risk your neck for these people."

Ryan drained the remainder of the beer from the can and tossed it.

Shelby continued, "You've gained their respect. People confide in those they respect that's why I want you to be the bridge between us and them." Shelby looked at his right-hand man, the one that went by the name John.

"Not sure what you expect of me."

Shelby looked across the yard and sniffed hard. "I expect you to put your ear to the ground, keep your eyes open. I imagine there are those among the group that would confide in you. You see, Ryan, I could stand here all day long and threaten them but it's not going to get me anywhere. Trying to find who's responsible for these deaths right now is like looking for a needle in a haystack. It's a waste of resources. But you! You could do it for me."

"If they wouldn't tell you when you were threatening them with a gun, what makes you think they would tell me?"

"You're not listening. They trust you."

"So you want me to act like a Trojan horse for you, so you can eventually weed out one individual and kill them?"

"No, this is not about killing, it's about bestowing my goodness upon the rest of the ones here who didn't act selfishly."

"Selfish? What, you think killing two people from a group that killed more than twenty of ours is selfish?"

"Okay, wrong choice of words." He eyed Ryan carefully. "But you have to understand. You would have never opened those gates without force."

Ryan scowled. "Oh so it's our fault?" He paused. "If someone breaks into a store is the owner at fault because they locked their doors?"

Shelby motioned with his cigarette. "These are dangerous times."

"So that gives you the right to burst in and kill people and take what we have?"

Shelby stood up and squared off to him. "I don't care what you think is right or wrong in this situation. It is what it is, and you will roll with it or be added to the pile over there," he said motioning with his eyes. "Now back to what I'm asking you to do. Will you do it or do I need to find someone more compliant?"

"No, I'll do it but I can't guarantee making progress. If whoever is doing this doesn't want to speak, they won't."

Shelby looked at the people then back at him. "Do what you can."

He turned to walk away.

"And what do I get out of it?" Ryan asked.

He heard Shelby chuckle before he turned back. "A businessman. I like that." He ran a hand over his face and regarded Ryan with a look of admiration. "Find out who's responsible before the day is out and you'll all eat today."

"You offered that deal to all of us."

"Okay then, bring me the person responsible and I will

ensure you don't have to do shifts around this place."

Ryan snorted, turned and walked back to work. Shelby was desperate and unhinged and that was a dangerous recipe for disaster.

* * *

Elliot was deeply troubled by what had unfolded. After Sean willingly gave information to Dallas, their zip ties were cut, and then they were strong-armed out of the bar and taken next door to a grimy auto repair shop. Outside there were multiple dilapidated vehicles lined up. Inside, the stench of grease and oil permeated. There were two rusted-out sedans on car stands, with the hoods popped as if the owner of the business had started work and gave up.

"Don't even think about trying to escape," Dallas said.

The door was shut behind them and locked in place.

There was no rear exit as the garage butted up against a steep rock face. There were two doors either side, one at the front and a two-vehicle entranceway, but they had three of their guys outside watching over the place.

Gary kicked an oil can across the floor. "Well this is

fucking great!"

"Steady there my friend, you're liable to blow a blood vessel," Damon said.

"Ah screw you!"

"Come on, Gary, it's not his fault," Elliot said.

"No, it's yours."

Elliot bristled pointing to his chest. "Mine?"

"Yeah, if you had just agreed to let us use the Jeep we would have been miles away from Lake Placid by now."

"Well first off, how were you going to fit everyone in that Jeep? You needed those horses. And second, it wasn't your damn vehicle to take."

Gary waved him off. "I'm not getting into this with you. Chances are we'll all be dead by the end of today."

Sean piped up, "No we won't. You heard him. We gave him the vehicle and her, he said he would let us go."

"Yeah, what the hell was you thinking?" Damon shouted at him.

"I was making damn sure we didn't die. You can thank me later."

"The fuck I will," Damon said turning away.

"Guys, this is not helping," Zach said. "We just need to figure out how to get out of here."

"We're not," Gary added in a pessimistic tone.

Elliot looked at Ella who had closed the hood on one of the vehicles and hopped up. For someone likely to be murdered later by Dallas and his crew, she was acting very calm and collected. He strolled over and hopped up beside her. She shot him a sideways glance.

"I'm sorry," she said with a soft voice.

"You have nothing to be sorry about."

"But I got you into this mess."

"No you didn't," Elliot replied. "People are people. Even if you weren't with us, they would have stopped us and probably killed us by now. In fact you might have saved us."

She snorted. "Look at you all positive and shit."

He smiled and glanced over at Gary who was rooting through a toolbox. "Someone has to be. I have a wife and kids to get back to and this sure as hell isn't going to be my final resting place."

He reached into his pocket for a cigarette then realized he didn't have any.

"Any of you got a smoke?"

"No, I'm all out," Damon replied.

"Guy outside took mine when he frisked us," Zach said.

Elliot nodded and let out a heavy sigh. "Well, I figure it will take them a few hours before they're back, well, that's if they leave immediately. If they return empty-handed there is a fifty-fifty chance we'll die. If they come back with horses, we might be in luck."

"What?" Gary said. "You act as if we are getting out of here."

"I am. Maybe not alive but I'm not going to make killing me easy."

Zach chuckled. "Either of those cars got keys inside?" he asked before taking a look.

"Even if they did, they are too new."

"New?" He broke off a piece of rusted metal from a

side panel.

"It's not what it's made of, it's when it was made," Damon said.

At the rear of the garage Gary sounded all pleased with himself.

"Aha!" Gary said pulling out a large wrench and swinging it around. "Here, catch!" He tossed it to Elliot, and he caught it in his left hand. "There's more where that came from."

Zach and Damon went over to see what they could find. Elliot handed the oversized wrench to Ella. Meanwhile Sean looked on with an expression of confusion. "What the hell are you planning on doing? Are you really going to go up against armed men with wrenches? You are going to get us all killed. No, I say we do nothing. Wait until this Dallas guy gets back and he'll let us go. Just like he promised."

"He's not letting us go, Sean," Elliot said.

"And you would know this because?"

"Ugh, does anyone else want to explain it to him?"

Elliot hopped off the Ford sedan and strolled to the back of the garage and started looking at what other items could be used as weapons. There was a can of WD-40, a hacksaw, pliers, screwdrivers, hammers, booster cables, masking tape and portable drills.

"I think we can come up with something."

Sean muscled his way past Damon and Zach. "Elliot, I don't agree with this."

Elliot tossed a hammer around in his hand without looking at him. "Who said you did?"

"This is ludicrous."

He turned and without even a flicker of a smile he replied, "No. It's pure survival! All we need to do is get one rifle off them and we can take out the other two. But we need to act fast before they get back."

"Ella can lure them."

She looked at Damon.

"Well you did say you'd done that before."

"Yeah, but I hardly think that's going to work now."

"No, don't bother, I have an idea," Elliot said.

"Damon, you still got that lighter on you?"

"Yeah."

"Here's what I want you to do."

Chapter 9

Shortly after ten in the morning Rayna found herself on the west side. While grocery stores, hotels, restaurants and cafés were the first to be hit by looters — not all the homes in the area had been searched. There were hundreds of them out there and while Elliot and Gary searched surrounding towns, Rayna stayed local. She never told Elliot because he would have only blown his top and said it was too dangerous. But she didn't want to man the blockades, and it didn't feel right to do nothing when there was a gold mine of stash to be found.

For the first time in a long while Jill had decided to tag along. It had given them time to talk. Jill was still guarded, but Rayna was beginning to notice small changes. She figured that was because they were planning on leaving Lake Placid.

Rayna kicked garbage out of the way as she pushed her way through the rear door of a house. With the power grid down and no more services running, homes and streets were littered with all manner of shit.

"What a stench!" she said, sweeping her AR-15 behind her as she tied a red handkerchief around her nose and mouth so she didn't have to inhale the smell of death. It wasn't just garbage but people who had died from illness or violence. According to Elliot, it was estimated that up to 90 percent of Americans would be dead within 12 to 18 months due to starvation, disease, and social breakdown. That figure seemed high but after considering that police were powerless to react, and they hadn't seen the National Guard due to a breakdown in communication and mobilization, it made sense. Of course then there was the concern of safe water. Not everyone would have been familiar with how to purify water and without basic medication; it didn't take long for the weak and ill informed to die.

"I'm just saying it's for the best," Jill said continuing the conversation they'd had about leaving town. "We can't survive another winter. You saw all those people who died from pneumonia, and just look around you, there has been a complete collapse of sanitation. I'm surprised we haven't ended up with hepatitis or some unknown disease yet."

"No, I know it's for the best. I just thought we'd see a change in the country by now."

"Me too," she replied, picking up a box and tossing it across the room.

Jill knocked over several large chairs and waded through the cesspool that was once home to someone. Rayna started rooting through cupboards. Most were empty, those that weren't had food that had turned rotten. Jill opened a cupboard then screamed, jumping back and nearly losing her footing.

Rayna spun around. "What is it?"

She cringed. "A rat."

"You should have caught it, we could have made stew out of that."

Jill raised an eyebrow, and Rayna laughed.

They ventured further into the house, glancing at the

various photo frames scattered on the ground. Someone had been through the place with a spray can and left graffiti that read: SCREW THIS LIFE. That was mild compared to the other vulgar phrases.

"I think we should try another house," Jill said shaking her head in disgust. Rayna wasn't through yet. She climbed the staircase to the second floor and eased open each door. The bathroom was vile with feces spilling over the brim of the toilet, most of it caked dry. Blue bottle flies buzzed around it. She felt her gag reflex kick in. She spent a minute or two in a child's bedroom before entering the master bedroom that belonged to the parents. As soon as the door swung wide she wished she hadn't entered. A woman dressed in nothing but a nightgown was hanging from the back of her closet door by an exercise band, her skin purple and gray. On the other side of the room was a male with a knife in one hand and his palms facing upwards. He'd slit both of his wrists. The carpet was drenched in blood. But that wasn't the worst of it. A pair of small feet stuck out from the closet. There was no movement and it was clear from the color of the child's skin that she was dead. She didn't dare take a look. Rayna backed out bumping into Jill.

"What is it?" Jill asked.

She closed the door behind her. "You don't want to know. Let's go."

They made their way down and continued on to the next home. They searched through seven homes before Rayna got a sense they were being watched. At first it was subtle. Nothing more than a gut instinct. She hadn't seen anyone and there was no telling if they were a threat but that didn't matter. Two more houses and they would call it a day. Inside a carrier bag they'd collected some cans of food. It wasn't much, four cans of peas, some beans, and peaches.

"Gary won't be going to the compound," Jill said.

"I didn't say he would."

"But you know Elliot will try to convince him."

"Is that a bad thing?"

"It's too risky."

"So is walking into a FEMA camp."

"You act as if they're the enemy."

"Jill. You're tossing the dice. It's a fifty-fifty chance."

"Well I would rather side with the government than unknowns."

"The government is an unknown. We have never experienced a situation like this. We have no idea what kind of operation they have running or who they will let in. Just because they are running a camp, it doesn't mean everyone is going to be let inside. Think about it. Who would you let inside first?"

"Soldiers, doctors, engineers, scientists."

"That's right, they are going to have a screening process. And unless you have skills that can be useful, chances are they won't be letting you in."

"You don't know that."

"Of course I do," Rayna said. "It's common sense. Hell, it's what Ted Murphy tried to do here before he died. He focused on those with skills. Hunters, military personnel. It will be the same down there."

"Then it will be the same with the compound you want to go to."

"Actually no it won't. Maggie said they have their own screening process and it didn't matter if you aren't skilled."

Jill snorted. "Right. And you think we're stupid for placing our trust in FEMA."

"I didn't say you're stupid." Rayna's brow pinched. "What is the deal with you? Years ago you would have never thought I was against you and then this shit blows up between us and you think I'm your enemy."

Jill dipped her head.

"I'm sorry," she replied softly.

Rayna placed a hand on her arm. "You're my closest friend. And you always will be. Nothing's changed that."

Jill looked embarrassed. She was just about to reply when they heard the echo of gunfire. Rayna immediately brought up her rifle, as did Jill. A few seconds of hesitation and Rayna started moving. "Let's head out."

"I won't argue with that," Jill replied.

They hurried through the house and made their way out into the fenced backyard. As they exited and turned south on Nash Street, a woman cried out. The scream was gut wrenching. Rayna turned and Jill shook her head. "No."

"But—"

"No!" Jill said.

Another scream pierced the air and they saw a half-naked blond woman dash out of a home six houses down. She bolted across the street and disappeared around the side of a house. Several guys followed seconds after.

Jill and Rayna ducked behind a stalled vehicle and Rayna looked through the window. More screams. Jill shuffled down to the next vehicle trying to put distance between herself and the commotion. Rayna followed but the screams just got worse.

"We should help."

"She's not our responsibility," Jill yelled back.

"If that was Lily…"

"It's not. Now let's go."

Rayna clenched her jaw and snuck another peek over the car hood before sliding over to Jill as the screams intensified.

"Listen to me. You go. If I'm not back in an hour you know where to find me."

Jill grabbed her by the arm as Rayna got up to leave. "Elliot wouldn't want this."

"I make the decisions, not him."

With that said she jumped up and ran at a crouch down the street until she got to the next corner that fed into the alley she'd seen the woman run down. She risked taking a look before wheeling around the corner and hauling ass. She followed the noise of wailing to a home six buildings down. Her eyes scanned her field of vision. There was no one there. She hurried down the next alley until she arrived at the home where the screaming was coming from. Crouched down she pressed her back against the fence. Her pulse was racing. She readjusted the grip on the rifle and counted down to calm her nerves. 5, 4, 3, 2, 1. She ran the numbers in her head again and was about to enter the rear gate that led up to the house when Jill appeared. Rayna waited for her to catch up.

"I can't believe you are doing this," Jill said.

"Listen, just wait here, watch my back while I go in. If anyone comes, get inside."

Jill didn't respond as Rayna hurried in.

The screams subsided and all that could be heard was gentle sobbing as Rayna entered the rear door. On first inspection she didn't see anyone inside but she could hear her. She looked back toward the gate and saw Jill who had stepped inside so she wasn't out in the open. She had positioned herself behind the fence so that if anyone came through the gate she could take them out. Being in position was one thing, trusting her to kill was another. Rayna moved forward clearing each room as she went until she entered the living room.

Kneeling on a floor covered in newspaper was the woman with her back turned toward her.

"Ma'am. Ma'am, you okay?" she asked without approaching her.

The woman didn't answer but continued to sob. Rayna took one more look down the corridor before she entered and made her way over. She placed a hand on her shoulder and the woman flinched.

"It's okay. You're safe."

The sobbing slowly morphed into laughter, then she turned. "Good because you're not."

It happened so fast; two men entered the room with Glocks raised.

"Put it down," one of them said in a hard tone. He was a black dude with an American flag bandanna wrapped around his head. The other male was tattooed and had dreadlocks. "Slowly," he said. "Trixie, grab her gun, and well done, that was some first-class acting."

She squealed with delight. "Getting better each time," she replied rising to her feet and pulling up her top to cover her exposed breasts. Her arms were riddled with dark puncture marks. *An addict. Great,* Rayna thought.

"Look, just take what you want and I'll be out of your hair."

After the woman took her rifle, the black guy stepped forward closing the gap between them. "But I want you," he said before lunging forward and licking the side of her face. She struck him with her left fist knocking him to the ground and was about to attack the next man when the woman raised the rifle to her head.

"Go on. Do it, bitch. Just give me a reason." She cackled as the black guy got up from the ground wiping blood from his lip. He was about to lash out when they heard a commotion outside. Several rounds were fired in rapid succession.

"Spider. Go check it out," the black guy said to the tattooed freak.

Once he exited the room, Rayna's wrists were bound with rope.

Two more shots echoed outside, then the sound of boots heading down the hallway.

"What was it, Spider?" the black guy asked.

Jill spun around the corner with her rifle raised. "I'm afraid your friend is out of action, now put it down and back away from her."

A smile flickered on Rayna's face. She'd underestimated her.

The black guy didn't bat an eye. He was already standing behind Rayna when Jill appeared in the doorway. He brought a knife up to Rayna's throat. "I don't think so. You put it down or I'll slice her from ear to ear."

"Don't do it, Jill."

The guy pressed the blade and nicked her skin to let her know he wasn't playing. A bead of blood streaked down Rayna's throat disappearing below her shirt. Jill kept her gun trained on the psychotic-looking tweaker who was struggling to hold the rifle. There was barely any meat on her arms.

"Put it down!" the woman cried.

Jill remained stoic and poised, her finger resting on the trigger.

"Take the shot, Jill."

The black guy pushed the knife edge into Rayna's

larynx causing her to cry out. If she just had a free hand, she might have got out of it but with her hands restrained it was impossible. She felt him press the blade harder against her skin

Seconds seemed like minutes as Jill contemplated what to do.

Instead of taking the shot she backed away, disappearing behind the corner.

"Jill!"

The sound of boots pounding the floor grew distant.

The black guy laughed. "Now that was a smart lady. You really should pick better friends. Now let's get the fuck out of here," he said pushing her forward. He shoved Rayna out of the room into the hallway and they made their way to the rear of the home. At the back entrance sprawled on the ground with blood seeping out of his head was Spider.

"Shit, Spider, you dumb idiot!"

They stepped over him and Rayna noted that his rifle had been taken. Outside she now got a better picture of what had happened. Two more men had entered the rear gate and had been plowed down by Jill. Blood trailed away from their bodies. Their weapons were gone. All she could hope was that Jill had gone to get help. The black guy kept a firm grip on Rayna as he checked the road both ways before exiting the rear yard.

"What do you want with me?" Jill asked.

"You'll find out soon enough, now shut up and keep walking."

As they ambled up the road to another house, the two of them talked about getting a new batch of meth. Rayna learned the woman's name was Trixie and she called him Boomer. He pushed her on and they continued down the road while the meth head behind kept watch over them. Every now and again Boomer would tap his handgun against Rayna's waist to let her know that if she tried anything she was dead.

The sound of music could be heard — a light thumping noise of a bass drum. As they got closer to an apartment block, two hefty individuals were standing outside. They wore light jackets and had thick beards.

"Is Doc in?" Boomer asked.

"Who's asking?"

"Tell him Boomer comes bearing gifts."

One of the guys got on a radio and a voice crackled over it to give them the go-ahead. Inside it smelled of urine. Draped over the steps on the way up were several addicts completely out of it. Needles stuck out of their arms and they looked completely spaced out. They climbed two flights of steps before entering a darkened hallway. At the far end were three more hard-nosed individuals smoking joints.

One of them clasped hands with Boomer and let him inside.

Music reverberated as they entered a cloud of smoke. The rancid, musty smell of marijuana lingered in the air. Inside, cans of beer and bottles of wine littered the floor. In the living area were four naked women sitting around a bald white guy who was wearing nothing more than a fur coat, gold chains, brown slippers, and dirty white underwear. It was a gross sight. The smell in the place was atrocious. He was leaning over a table snorting up a line of coke when he locked eyes with Boomer.

He grinned revealing a gold grill on his teeth.

"Boomer. About time."

"I brought you that payment."

He shoved Rayna forward onto her knees.

Chapter 10

Gary shoved Elliot into the garage door making it clatter and shake. Both were yelling at the top of their voices, blaming one another. Moving from the front to the rear, Elliot threw Gary across the ground. He tumbled and slammed into a pile of cardboard boxes filled with car parts.

The sound of a key in the lock, and then a twist.

A door swung open and one of the men entered with his rifle raised.

"Hey! Enough!"

The others egged them on. Chaos, confusion, it was all just a distraction. Damon pulled the WD-40 and the lighter from behind his back. With one flick, a flame ignited and he sprayed the flammable liquid in the guard's direction. A three-foot flame shot out while Zach tackled the guy from the other side. The gun went off and the two outside raced towards the entrance. Damon had already shifted position, while Zach struggled to get the gun off the guy. It let off another round, shattering a window near Gary's head. The guard's pals entered with weapons drawn but it was pointless. Damon launched himself off a steel cabinet, plunging a screwdriver into the throat of one of them and bringing him down. Before the other one could respond Ella cracked him on the jaw with the wrench. The attack was fast, brutal and deadly.

Ella continued beating the man to death until Gary intervened.

"Hey! He's dead. That's enough."

She straightened up with brain matter on her face. Ella wiped it with the back of her sleeve. Zach hadn't managed to wrestle the rifle away from the guy but he'd managed to keep him on the ground. Elliot pried the weapon out of his hand, breaking his finger in the process, then without hesitation fired a round into the man's skull. Damon scooped up a rifle, and Gary took the other one. They gathered ammo and remained inside for a minute or so peering out the grimy windows to see if anyone else had heard. There was no movement. No one else came to back up their comrades.

"Let's move out," Elliot said leading the way.

Cautiously they darted out, heading south on Broadway. Within minutes of being on the road they came under attack. Rounds speared through some of the stalled cars and windows of nearby stores, driving them in the opposite direction. The three of them returned fire.

Walls were peppered with rounds, and the sound of gunfire dominated.

"If something feels too good to be true, it never fails to be," Damon hollered.

Not everyone in Dallas's group had gone on a road trip to see if there were horses. A large number of men and women had been patrolling the street around the Rusty Nail or making their way back after hearing gunfire.

Elliot and the others made it to the Fire Department building and hurried into the parking lot, and cut through woodland to Depot Street. Every few yards they had to take cover behind trees, stalled vehicles or buildings to return fire. They sprinted across a set of train tracks and dashed into a residential area.

"There are too many of them. We need to split up," Gary said.

"No!" Elliot yelled. "We stick together."

"Then we die together," he replied.

Though he complained, they worked together to hold them off as they ran for what felt like half an hour, stopping and starting.

"I'm out of ammo!" Damon yelled.

Elliot reached into his pocket and tossed a magazine to him.

* * *

At the same time, in Lake Placid, Rayna remained on her knees while Boomer explained to Doc what he wanted in exchange for her. Now she'd seen a lot of trading being offered over the past six months but for people? That was a first.

"I don't know she looks a little old for my liking."

Boomer came over. "Oh no, she's perfect. Look at the meat on this woman. There is plenty of flesh to sink your teeth into."

Cannibalism had been a topic of conversation in the past few months but was that what he was referring to? She learned fast it wasn't.

"No, she's got at least twenty years on these gals," Doc said slapping the ass on one of the women. They all looked doped up. Their arms and legs were riddled with needle marks.

"No, I'm telling you, this is a fine bit of ass."

"Alright, let's see the merchandise."

He nodded, a look of wild excitement in his eyes. "Sure thing."

With that he turned to Rayna, took out a knife from a sheath at his waist and cut down the front of her top. He made a large tear and then tore it open, slicing through her bra to expose her. She tried resisting but with her hands bound behind her, all she could do was kick him and that didn't last long. One strike to the face and she was seeing stars. Blood started dripping from her nose across her lip.

"Hey! Don't bruise the merchandise."

"Yeah, yeah. So, what do you think?" Boomer replied.

Rayna groaned, her dignity vanished as Doc came over and manhandled her breasts. "Not bad. Not bad at all. How old are you?" he asked. Rayna spat blood in his face and told him to go fuck himself. That only made him laugh. He licked the blood from his hand and sucked it between his brown messed-up teeth. "Oh I think she will fit in just right here. I like a woman with fire." He breathed in deeply. "I'll give you ten grams for her."

"Ten? She is worth more than that. I want thirty or there is no deal."

Doc laughed and walked back over to his seat. He dropped down and took out a bag of crystal meth from below the table and started weighing out the white crystals. "Fifteen and I throw in ten grams of weed."

"I've got plenty of weed. I need meth."

"Then I guess you're going to have to make your

own."

"Yeah, with what? You took all the ingredients."

"Travel to another town."

Boomer eyed him with a look of disgust.

"Twenty-five grams."

Doc leaned back, placing both arms around his women like he was king.

"Sorry. It's called supply and demand. This shit is in real demand right now. People want to get fucked up and float away to their happy place."

"This is bullshit." Boomer jabbed the floor. "Twenty, or I walk right now."

The bald-headed prick ran his tongue around his lips while looking at Rayna.

"Okay. Twenty it is."

"And I get the marijuana."

"Don't push it," Doc replied as he went about filling up a bag with twenty grams. Behind her Rayna could hear Trixie snickering to herself.

She leaned in real close to Rayna's ear and whispered,

"Oh the doc is going to enjoy you." She laughed again but her laughter turned to cries when Rayna jerked her head back and head-butted her.

"Bitch!"

She grabbed Rayna but Boomer pushed Trixie back. "She's not our property now."

He pushed her over to the couch and waited patiently, bouncing from one foot to the next, for Doc to give him the goods. Doc handed over the baggie and waved him off.

"Now go."

Boomer frowned. "What about the marijuana?"

"Get the fuck out of my sight before I put a bullet in both of you!"

They nodded, backed up quickly and squabbled over the meth as they exited. As soon as the door slammed closed, Doc leaned forward and took another hit of coke.

"Darlin', you're going to like it here. Two meals a day. As much coke as you can snort, and the best part — you get to enjoy me."

He reached over and ran his hand down her body. "Now let's get you out of those clothes."

* * *

Jill had no intentions of leaving her behind. She realized the odds were against her so she backed off and kept her distance. She'd seen them exit and watched those two assholes lead her into that shithole of an apartment block. Now, she observed the apartment from inside a home across the street. Jill had taken a long-range rifle from one of the two dead men.

Six months ago she would have run for her life, and allowed fear to rule, but that was the old her, before being pushed into a corner by her life, before being made to feel less than a woman by her husband. She already knew how to shoot a weapon, Gary had taken her to a firing range countless times. It made him feel secure knowing that she could use a weapon just in case anyone broke into the house while he was on shift.

When she saw the two tweakers leaving the apartment block without Rayna she hurried down the steps and followed them while keeping her distance. They moved quickly, threading their way around stalled vehicles. The rail-thin woman bounced around like an overly excited kid in a candy store.

They walked about six blocks before they entered a run-down house where the windows were shattered. Jill gave the street another glance before quietly heading inside. She could hear them talking.

"Twenty grams. I can't believe that asshole gave you that for her."

"I know. I would have accepted five. Did you hear me? Twenty or I walk. The look on his face."

"Come on, give me some of that," the woman said.

"Hold on. Hold on. How about you give me something first?"

"Boomer. After. I need it now."

"After."

"But—"

"Bitch, just do it now."

She heard a sigh and then a table being jerked around.

Jill looked down at the glass on the floor and made sure not to step on any of the fragments. She pressed on into the house, the AR-15 raised and ready. As she came around the corner that fed into the kitchen, she found the guy with his pants around his ankles and the woman bent over the table. He was grunting, and she was groaning. He was in the middle of having sex when she crept up behind him and pressed the gun to the back of his head.

"Don't fucking move!"

He stopped thrusting while she reached around and removed the rifle that belonged to Rayna. She tossed it out into the hallway while keeping her gun on him.

"Where is she?"

The guy laughed. "Probably laid on her back somewhere being used and abused."

Jill lowered the gun and squeezed a round, shooting him in the ass. He let out a scream. He collapsed to the ground, his genitals flapping around as he groped his bloody ass.

"Ah, stop whining. It's just a flesh wound," she said

turning the gun on the woman who was hiking up her underpants.

"You! What apartment is she in?"

"Don't tell her," Boomer said, but it was too late.

"3C."

Without missing a beat Jill turned the rifle on him and fired another round into his leg then adjusted quickly as the woman lunged. "Aha, no, I don't think so. Get over there with him." She crossed the room. "On the floor."

Jill noticed the bag of meth on the counter.

"Was that what you exchanged her for?"

They didn't respond. Jill picked it up and tossed it at the girl.

"Go on, snort it."

"What?" she asked.

"A few minutes ago you were begging for some. Go on. Snort it!"

"But—"

"Do it!" Jill bellowed.

The guy was groaning in agony and complaining

about having been shot twice as if she wasn't aware. She watched as the woman snorted some off her hand.

"And the rest," Jill said.

She did some more but that wasn't enough.

"Snort the entire bag."

"But—"

Jill fired a round to the right of her. "The next one goes in you."

Quickly the woman began snorting as much of it as she could. Watching her made Jill sick. She hated drugs. She hated what they did to people. What people were willing to do for them. Once the woman had snorted it all, her eyes were wild and her body was shaking. The woman started to laugh. At first it was mild then it turned into a full belly laugh. "Oh you are screwed. You aren't getting her back. He's the doc."

"Then I have no need for you two."

Jill fired a round into the woman's chest, killing her instantly, then turned the gun on the guy who had his hands out. "Please. I can get her back."

"Not in that state you can't." She pulled the trigger and a round punctured his skull. "I hate tweakers," she said turning and walking out. It felt good to take control. For so long she'd just sat on the sidelines being controlled by fear. She was done with that shit.

Jill made her way back to the house across from the apartment and returned to the window. She took a moment to gather her thoughts. Her eyes roamed the room and then she glanced at the two guards outside the apartment. There was a chance one of them would raise the alarm but she had to take that risk. She slid open the window, pushed over a computer table and cleared it off. She then brought up the long-distance rifle, got on the table and rested the muzzle on the edge of the window frame. She recalled what Gary had taught her about handling, aiming and controlling her breathing. It wasn't far away. Two shots, that was all it required. The first would be easy enough, the second tricky but possible. She brought the scope up to her eye and put the first guy in the crosshair. She took a deep breath and exhaled slowly as she touched the fleshy part of her finger against the trigger.

The gun let out a crack and one of the men dropped.

A few seconds was all she needed to adjust her aim as the other guy registered the attack. "That's it, reach down to see if he's alive, you idiot!"

Another gunshot echoed, and the round punctured the man's temple.

Not wasting any time she dropped the rifle, picked up the AR-15 and hurried out of the house and across the road. Gunfire was so commonly heard, she knew if he had any other men inside, they probably wouldn't come out to see what the commotion was about. She planned on using that to her advantage.

Bringing up the rifle, she pulled open the door to the apartment block and entered.

Chapter 11

The warm, rancid smell of piss wafted in Jill's face as she entered the apartment block. Her pulse raced as she slowly but surely made her way along the darkened corridor heading for the stairwell. A groan came from farther down, an addict lying in his own vomit, probably overdosed. There was graffiti all over the cream-colored walls and unknown puddles of brown liquid on the floor. She stepped over it grimacing. The state of the world had become so bad, and it had all taken place in a matter of weeks. Since the lights had gone out, her world had changed dramatically. Not only had she learned her husband had been cheating on her with her best friend, but all the plans that she had for adoption had gone out the window. She'd always wanted kids and now it seemed like it would never happen. Jill tightened her grip on the AR-15 and used her foot to push open a grimy door leading into the stairwell.

Though she tried to remain focused, her thoughts kept drifting to what Rayna had said about their friendship. *Nothing has changed.* In her mind everything had changed and yet she was starting to realize that perhaps it wasn't Rayna she was angry with, maybe it was herself and allowing Gary to take her for a ride. It was confusing because she knew that Gary loved her by the way he treated her when they were alone. It wasn't the physical intimacy but the things he did for her — he'd take time out of his day and do things she wanted to do even though she knew he hated going to theater productions or dancing. But that was him — he'd always been loving, maybe that's why the news from Rayna blindsided her. Of course she wasn't stupid, Rayna was beautiful, far more beautiful than she was. But still, it had pained her to know that Gary felt he couldn't get his needs met with her.

Jill glanced up the steps and traversed her way over numerous drug addicts. One grabbed her leg and for a brief second she nearly squeezed the trigger, instead she slammed him in the face with the butt and knocked the guy out.

At the top of the stairs she peered through the glass. There was no one there, at least that she could see. Easing the door open she kept the rifle low and cut the corner with her head. *In. Out.* Gary had shown her how to do it without being seen.

There were three of them standing at the far end of the corridor. While they weren't holding weapons in their hands, she noticed the rifles strapped over their shoulders. It wouldn't take them long to spin them around and return fire. Could she take out all three without being shot? She wasn't wearing a vest. Jill took a deep breath and closed the door contemplating what Gary would have done.

On one hand she had considered traipsing back to the bunker and getting Jesse and Maggie but even if she jogged she was looking at a good forty minutes, and who knew what horrors were being inflicted upon Rayna? No, she couldn't leave her.

Jill glanced down at the rifle. What if three rounds wasn't enough? It all depended on where the bullet hit. She gritted her teeth and nodded a few times before pulling open the door and thrusting out into the corridor with the gun raised. It took the men less than two seconds to register her presence but that was all she needed to squeeze, once, twice, a third time and then she just kept squeezing moving forward, keeping them in the crosshair. Only one of them managed to swing his weapon around and unload two shots before he fell, the others collapsed and she continued squeezing off rounds until she was sure they were dead.

Jill pulled the magazine and tossed it, then palmed another in and prepared for the unexpected. Whoever was inside the room had no idea what was going on outside. They would have heard the gunfire but that might have come from their own men. She hurried down the corridor until she found herself looking at apartment 3C.

For all she knew there could be twenty men on the other side.

This wasn't about heroics, it was about getting in and out. She tried the door but it was locked. She pulled back but not before scooping up one man's guns. Jill hurried back to the stairwell expecting others to come. That's when she got an idea. She laid down the rifles, grabbed one of the addicts who wasn't conscious and dragged him to the corner of the stairwell. She tore her top and lay back beside him, covering the loaded rifle beneath her using a dirty blanket laid on the ground. She sank her hands into whatever brown gunk was spread across the floor and wiped it through her hair. Her gag reflex kicked in and she wanted to throw up.

Voices.

Several men.

"Fuck. Go. Don't stand here. Go see."

She covered the rifle and leaned against the addict as if she'd taken one too may pills. Drool dripped out the corner of her mouth and she acted as if she was barely conscious.

The stairwell door burst open and two hulking guys

charged forward, glancing at her then inching towards the top of the stairwell. They were nervous. Certainly not ready to race down those stairs and engage in a gunfight but that was exactly what she was counting on. As they turned their backs, she pulled back the blanket, her finger ready on the trigger. Barely moving she raised it and without wasting another second squeezed aiming for their heads. One of the men collapsed beside her, the other toppled over the edge of the banister and vanished. A thud was the final sound of him leaving this world.

She waited a second to see if any more were coming. *No voices. Nothing.*

Jill rose to her feet using the blanket to wipe the shit — which she came to realize was vomit — from her face. Slipping back out into the corridor she moved with purpose, speed and confidence. Twenty steps down that corridor and another black guy came out.

The round struck him in the head as a look of astonishment spread on his face.

As soon as she reached the door, she peered around

and caught sight of naked women huddled together. Among them was Rayna. Rage welled up as she noticed a needle sticking out of her arm. "NO!" she blurted out as she stepped inside only to find herself confronted by a bald-headed asshole wielding a large revolver.

"Put it down," he commanded.

Jill knew the moment she dropped it he would kill her.

Her finger twitched on the trigger, keeping it aimed at him even as her eyes flicked over to Rayna. Rayna was barely conscious. Her eyes were glassy and void of emotion.

"What have you done to her?"

"Oh, you know her?" He chuckled. "Don't you worry about her. She's golden." He nudged again with his gun. "Lay the rifle down and you can join her. I'll take you to your happy place. There's more than enough of me to go around."

There in that moment she realized what Rayna meant to her.

How could she have held on to so much bitterness for

so long?

"Just let her go, and I'll leave."

He shook his head. "No can do. I paid for her."

"With a bag of drugs?" Jill met his gaze. "Is that what human life is worth?"

"Oh it's worth more than that. They were the ones who got the shabby deal."

Jill glanced at Rayna and the other women. Her eyes bounced around as the bald-headed freak started to get antsy. "Do you really want to take the risk? Is she really worth it?"

Jill snorted and chuckled a little. "You're right."

"I know."

"She's worth it."

With that said she pulled the trigger. The round punctured his stomach. He stumbled back but returned fire. The round caught her in the chest and her legs went out from beneath her. She let out a cry and squeezed again. One, then two, then three rounds, each one hitting their mark until he no longer moved.

Gasping for air, she gripped her chest, squeezing tight. The pain was excruciating. Searing hot. Her vision blurred and the sound of gunfire outside the building echoed. She opened and closed her mouth trying to get control but it was virtually impossible. She staggered to her feet, stumbling as she made her way over to Rayna. The first thing she did was pull the needle from her arm. Warm tears rolled down her cheeks.

"Come on darlin', wake up."

She slapped Rayna and her eyelids parted. Rayna muttered something but it was incomprehensible. Jill collapsed beside her, gripping her hand. A reel of memories flooded her mind; her childhood, her mother and father, meeting Gary, their wedding, life together, meeting Rayna and Elliot, laughter, tears, hope and a mixture of dreams — all of it blurred, a chaotic kaleidoscope of life. Her breathing became labored and with each inhale it was getting harder to stay conscious. Quickly darkness crept in at the corners of her eyes and she gripped Rayna's hand tight before her life slipped away.

* * *

Elliot led Dallas's group on one hell of a chase through the streets of Saranac Lake. By the time they managed to shake them they found themselves inside High Peaks Wine and Spirits in the late afternoon. The floors were covered with shattered bottles, discarded plastic cups, crumpled beer cans, empty boxes and all manner of trash. The shelves had been toppled.

Glass crunched below their boots as they sought cover. There wasn't one unopened bottle to be found in the place. Next to food, water and shelter, alcohol was like gold. If people weren't trying to survive each day, they were numbing out to escape the horrors of a collapsed society. Elliot and Gary leaned up against the front door and peered down the street from inside, fully expecting to see more of them.

Satisfied they weren't coming, they ventured further into the back. Even though it was still light out and daylight seeped in, it was dark inside. They walked into a storage area which once held hundreds of bottles of wine and beer. Now all that remained were empty pallets, boxes and crumpled cans.

Gary pushed the door closed behind them and locked it, then slid down with his back against it. All of them were sweating profusely and out of breath.

"Anyone hurt?" Damon asked.

"Nope."

"How you doing for ammo?" Elliot asked Gary.

"I'm out." He tossed the gun across the ground.

"Don't throw it, we might find ammo."

"Where? In your dreams?"

"We're gonna get out of here. We just need to wait for the sun to go down and then we'll head out."

"It's a long trek back home."

"Well I wasn't planning on going home. He has something of ours," Elliot said.

Gary frowned. "Are you kidding me? You want to go back?"

"Without that truck, or horses, we aren't going

anywhere. Not to a FEMA camp, not to Texas, nowhere."

Ella was looking around rooting through some boxes.

"Don't waste your time," Damon said. "It's all gone."

"Nothing else to do," she replied.

Gary focused his frustration on her. "Tell me something. For the last two months you've been killing their crew and avoiding them. Why and how?"

"Pretty obvious. They killed my parents."

"So you planned on killing them all?"

"That was the plan until Damon here showed up," she said with a grin on her face. She continued tossing boxes and searching.

"And how did you manage to last two months without them finding you?"

"I just did."

Gary looked at Elliot and shook his head. "No. Saranac isn't that big. There are a lot of them out there."

"And there are a lot of places to hide. I didn't sleep every night at my parents' place. You just happened to luck out yesterday. I would go back there when I could. I thought Damon was with them when they first showed up."

Damon nodded. "She nearly shot me in the face."

"Nearly? I would have."

There was silence except for her rooting around.

"Well damn, there we go!" She pulled from a box a small bottle of rum. "See, not everything is gone."

Zach made a gesture. "Toss it over here. I could use some of that right about now."

"Find your own. It's a small bottle."

"Hey, c'mon," Zach replied.

She unscrewed it and knocked it back, then smiled and handed it to him. Gary got up and scanned the area. He climbed up on a shelf and tried to look out a small window. "So come on then. Tell us where you stayed?"

"Everywhere. Some nights I slept under a bed, other nights I hid in a kitchen cupboard. Those were the worst. I only did that if they had chased me and I couldn't get out."

"If you can't get out, wait 'em out," Elliot said.

"Exactly!"

"Well as much as I would love to hang around here and swap stories, I'd prefer to get home," Gary said, jumping down and wiping grime from his jeans. The building they were inside was a huge house that had been converted into a place to sell liquor. It was an unusual-looking place but seemed to do the job. Ella wandered off through a door into another area. Elliot could hear her banging doors and crushing boxes.

"What on earth is she doing?" Sean asked

"Does it matter?" Damon replied.

"Well yeah, I don't want them finding us because she's making a shitload of noise."

Elliot motioned to Damon, and he headed out back to check on her. It soon quieted down.

Zach sat despondently looking at the ground.

"You okay?" Elliot asked.

"Yeah, I just wish I hadn't come out today."

"It's unavoidable. Maybe you escape these gangs today but what about tomorrow? Eventually they are gonna come knocking."

"It's just tiring," he said. "You'd think they would just work together instead of attack strangers."

"People still fear those they don't know."

"Sure but we don't know each other well."

Elliot shrugged. His mind drifted back to Fallujah and those his platoon had come across. Every day as they searched for insurgents he could see the look of fear in the faces of Iraqis.

Damon came out of the back room with a big grin on his face, his hands behind his back. "Ladies and gents, I do believe I have a solution to our problem."

With that said he whipped out two bottles of wine.

"Can you believe it?"

He held them high like he'd just won them in some raffle.

"Great, we can get drunk," Gary said shaking his head and walking back over to the shelving so he could take a look out of another window.

"Dude, you need to ease up. We are going to be here

for a while."

Gary hopped down. "We need to stay clear-headed."

"And we will. Now to get these babies open. Anyone got a corkscrew?"

"No need," Ella said coming out with two more bottles. She pulled out the wrench in her back pocket that she'd snagged from the garage and went over and began searching the shelves. "There we go." She picked up a piece of dirty rag on the ground and proceeded to twist out a screw that had come loose from the toppled shelving. Everyone watched curiously as she retrieved it, then stuck it in the cork and started working it in. She then stuck the bottle between her thighs, put two fingers around the screw and pulled until she got enough of the cork out. Then she used the wrench to work it loose.

"Creative. I'll give you that," Zach said. She took a big swig and handed a bottle to him. He quickly chugged it back. Although Gary was right about staying clear-headed, even Elliot wanted a couple of swigs. He joined them while Gary shook his head.

"We'll leave in a few hours. You have my word," Elliot said.

"No, we leave now," Gary replied.

"It's too dangerous."

"And you don't think it will be later?"

"At least we'll have the cover of darkness working for us."

He let out an exasperated sigh and ambled over to take a swig.

"Not bad, eh?" Ella said. He only took one gulp. Elliot didn't drink much more either. He slumped down against the ground. "Man, I could use a cigarette."

After leaving that message over the radio at the moment of capture, he assumed Rayna would be beside herself with worry, but at least she was safe.

Chapter 12

An hour later as the sun vanished beyond the horizon, light stabbed Rayna's eyes, and a chill made her shiver as she came around from the drug-induced coma. She cowered back unsure of where she was or what was happening. Someone was shining a flashlight directly in her eyes. She squinted and brought up a heavy arm to block the glare.

"What's going on?" she mumbled.

"You've been out a long time," a female voice replied.

Rayna felt a blanket slip off her. A partially dressed woman with long flowing hair and deep-set brown eyes looked back at her. She couldn't have been a day over twenty. Rayna's lips were dry. As the world around her crept in, she realized she was naked. That was when the memories hit her, fast and hard. The man they called Doc tearing her clothes off and the sexual assault that followed. Rayna cowered back thinking he had to be nearby but that fear soon subsided when her eyes fell upon him

Ten feet away the body of Doc lay motionless in a puddle of his own blood.

"It's okay. You're safe. He's dead."

Then she saw Jill.

"Jill?"

She reached for her and touched her cold hand.

"I'm sorry. She's dead too."

Rayna's mind tried to piece together the puzzle before her; the rifle laying five feet away, a trail of blood leading away to where she was. Jill had done this. She'd come for her. Tears started to roll down her cheeks. Her breathing became rapid, her focus blurred, and she felt like she was going to vomit.

"Slow down. Take it easy. You'll make yourself pass out," the girl said.

"Who are you?"

"Brianna Cooke."

"Where are the others?"

"Gone. When I woke they'd left. There's no one

outside except dead bodies."

"Where's my clothes?"

She gestured with her head to a pile over on a chair. "What's left of them are over there."

Rayna went to get up, but it felt like her legs had no bones in them. She wobbled and gripped the sofa before padding across the room and picking up torn panties. Another flash of memory. The only items that weren't ruined were her jeans and jacket. She slipped into them and grabbed her boots, then darted across the room and scooped up the rifle. The first thing she did was check the magazine before crossing over to Jill and crouching beside her. Her eyes were still open, locked in a death stare. Rayna ran her hand over her face to close them. She couldn't believe she was gone. Again she felt herself becoming choked up. What would she tell Gary? This was all her fault; if she hadn't gone to check on that girl — if she hadn't tried to help — if she'd only listened to Jill she would have been alive.

She deserved a proper burial, but no one buried the

dead now. It wasted too much energy. That wasn't Jill anymore. She was gone. At peace. Free from this hell. Before leaving she reached down and took off Jill's wedding and engagement bands and pocketed them. At least that was something she could give Gary.

While she was doing that Brianna got dressed.

"Where's home?" she asked.

"East side," Rayna replied without taking her eyes off Jill. "You?"

"Here. This was my home. This apartment."

"No, I mean before him."

"Here." She walked over to Doc and gave him a kick. "This man was my uncle. After my parents died, he moved in. I thought he wanted to help. Sick bastard!" She kicked his corpse three more times before spitting on him.

Rayna got up and started heading for the door.

"Can I come with you?" Brianna asked.

Rayna stopped and shook her head. "I can't help you."

"But I won't be a burden."

Rayna shook her head. Hours ago she would have

opened her arms to her. That was before this. She couldn't bear the guilt of losing anyone else. She stepped over dead bodies on her way out and made her way down the hall. Behind, she could hear Brianna following. She didn't say anything to her as she trudged down the dimly lit stairwell until she was outside and breathing fresh air. It was dark now. She had no idea how long she'd been out, only that she felt sick to her stomach. She steadied herself against the wall to catch her breath just as Brianna came out the door.

"You okay?" Brianna asked.

Rayna waved her off. "I'll be fine. I... just need a second."

Once she caught her breath Rayna began making the journey back home. Tears welled in her eyes. She could hardly comprehend that Jill was gone. Every few minutes she would look behind her thinking she was being followed. She kept her finger on the trigger. If anyone dared come near her, she wouldn't hesitate to shoot. The sound of a can kicked across the ground startled her and she spun around but no one was there. She picked up the pace heading north on Stevens Road. As she started to come down from the high of the drugs, her body ached. She could feel the pain of how he'd abused her. Rayna wiped tears from her cheeks. All she wanted to do was take a bath and scrub herself clean of that monster. Again she heard the sound of boots behind her. This time she broke into a jog and veered down Walsh Lane, then sprinted until she got to the Interlaken Inn. Rayna took cover behind the wall and waited. She heard someone running. Adjusting her grip on the rifle she readied herself. They couldn't have been twenty feet away when she brought the gun up. *C'mon!* She thought, finger on the trigger. As soon as they came around the corner she went to squeeze the trigger and then stopped.

"Whoa!" Brianna said.

"Why the hell are you still following me?" Rayna shouted in her face. "I could have killed you!"

"I know. I just don't have anywhere else to go."

"That's not my problem. Look around you. Find a

house. That's all we're doing."

"We're?" Brianna questioned her.

Rayna shook her head and pressed on. The girl caught up like an annoying fly.

"Please just go back," Rayna said. "There's nothing I can do to help you."

"I don't need help. I just need to be with someone."

"Well I'm not that person!" she stopped and yelled. The girl backed up a little. Rayna brought a hand up to her face and squeezed the bridge of her nose feeling a tension headache coming on. "You stick around me long enough, you'll wind up dead."

Jill's lifeless face flashed in her mind.

"I have nothing," Brianna said. "No family. Nothing."

"C'mon. You must have grandparents?" Rayna asked.

"Dead."

"Brothers, sisters?"

"Gone."

Rayna sighed and looked into the distance. Her mind was too overwhelmed with all the shit that just happened to deal with anyone else. All she wanted to do was get back to her kids. "If you slow me down…"

"I won't."

"You'll pull your weight."

Brianna nodded, a smile flickering on her face. "For sure."

Rayna motioned with her head. "C'mon. You know how to fire a gun?"

She pulled out the one that had belonged to Doc. "No, but I learn fast."

"Well start by pointing the barrel away from me."

Her eyebrows shot up. "Oh, sorry!"

They hurried on; unaware of the desperate faces looking at them from behind dirty windows.

Chapter 13

In the early hours of that evening, a large crowd had gathered outside the walls of New Hope Springs. Frank Shelby and his brother John watched intently from the top of the closest watchtower while his men performed checks on the travelers who'd heard the broadcast. There had to have been eighty, ninety, maybe over a hundred. None of them were allowed in unless they handed over their weapons. Of course, unlike the FEMA camps, they were told it was only precautionary and once they had been vetted to make sure they weren't a threat, they would get them back. He wasn't lying either. He wanted more men patrolling the perimeter. 650 acres was a lot of ground to cover and he figured they'd need at least a hundred people working around the clock providing security.

"How are you going to control this, Frank?" John said, unconvinced by his brother's ideas.

"Just like I've controlled our group. One at a time."

"You're letting in too many. They could be a threat."

"They could, however, without weapons they're just lions without teeth."

"But you said—"

"I know what I said. Relax, brother. It's early days. There are going to be some growing pains. I know there will be a few bad apples among the bunch but we'll weed them out."

John laughed. "You can't even weed out whoever is killing our men."

"Two. That's all. After today, I don't think there will be more."

"And if there is?"

He slapped him on the back and took a puff on his cigar. "Then we'll handle it. Like we always do." He blew smoke rings into the air. "Do you remember what you said when I told you we were going to break in here and take over?"

"Yeah, I said you were mad."

"And look where we are. Standing head and shoulders above them like kings."

"But for how long?"

"For as long we don't lose our shit." He gripped him by the collar. "It's all a matter of leverage." He shoved him up against the edge of the watchtower. "It doesn't take much to push a man over the edge. Right now we need more people. And this is a beautiful sight."

"And what happens when we fill out this place, but others come wanting in?"

"Then they are going to have one hell of a war on their hands."

John shook his head. "I don't know, brother. I don't like it."

"You're not supposed to. How did the founding fathers gain support for the constitution? Huh? How did they rally people around them?"

John said nothing.

"By promising them a bill of rights would be established. We are standing on the precipice of a new age, John. People's rights have been stripped. Whether that was by North Korea or by their own government, it doesn't matter. They are desperate, lost and looking for hope. I'm going to give them that, and in return they will give me their support."

John snorted. "You hope."

"Of course I do. Without hope, how would we have taken this place? Hope is what keeps us going. It's what gets people up in the morning. It's what makes men bleed for you even though they don't really know what they're fighting for."

"And what are we fighting for?"

Frank frowned. "After all this time you don't know what we are fighting for?"

"I just want to hear you say it."

"America. Freedom."

"But you are disarming these people."

He raised a finger. "No. FEMA is disarming. We are merely holding onto their firearms temporarily until they're established here. There's a big difference. It's

FEMA who is ordering people to work for them. These people are all going to willingly work with us. Do you understand? This is not about lording over them, it's about nurturing and leading and showing them what this great nation can be under true leadership."

They continued to watch the stream of people fill up the east courtyard. Frank placed a hand on his brother's shoulders. "Dad would have been proud."

"Are you sure about that?"

Frank glared at his brother. Over the past few months he'd become concerned for his mental well-being. He was starting to mistrust him. Before he'd been all gung-ho but when it came down to brass tacks, he wasn't sure he was cut out for the large responsibility that lay before them. This was nothing compared to what he had in mind. He didn't just have plans to survive, oh no, he wanted to dominate the great state of Texas. He wasn't greedy but for years, long before the EMP, he had ideas of how he could change the state for the better. Now it was like life was handing it to him on a platter. He sure as hell wasn't going to screw it up.

Down below several people argued. Frank got on the radio to find out what was going on.

"Report in."

"We got a group who won't give up their arms."

"Don't let them in. I'll be down to speak with them."

"I told you," John said in a self-assuring manner.

"Watch and learn, brother, watch and learn."

Frank made his way down and crossed the courtyard. A couple of his men escorted him past the long lines and through a crowd to where three refugees dressed in hunting gear stood looking defiant.

"Allow me to introduce myself. I'm General Shelby, though you can call me Frank."

It was all about being personal.

"You work for the government?" one of them piped up.

"Hell no. I have no problem with you guys coming in with those weapons but as you can see what we are offering here is far better than what is outside these walls.

So if you wish to be a part of it, you are going to have to either leave them outside the wall or hand them over. Either way you're getting them back. You decide what you feel more comfortable doing. Tell these gents, and they'll let you in."

He cast his glance over the rest. "That goes for all of you."

Frank turned and walked away knowing that was all that needed to be said. It wasn't a matter of restricting them but giving them options and letting them know they were in control, or at least giving them that perception.

Chapter 14

Dallas Jones went ballistic, kicking over chairs, swiping bottles off the bar and turning over tables. He swung at one of his men, his fist connecting with bone. Like an unruly child with no control over his emotions, he berated his close circle of friends. Everything had been going perfect that morning. After heading out to the ranch to gather what horses were available, he thought things were looking up. Not only had he gained a vehicle and got that bitch, he was on his way to retrieve a large selection of horses. It would make patrolling the town a hell of a lot easier. Since the lights had gone out they hadn't been able to snag a reliable means of transportation and with his group growing by the day, it only made sense to find horses. He just didn't think they would be in his own backyard.

"How the hell did you let them get away?" he bellowed.

Dallas paced back and forth in front of them. Each head hung low. They'd already given him several weak ass excuses. Beyond blaming each other, they didn't have a valid reason. Now had it been anyone else, he would have let it slide. The three men they'd killed were new to his group — they meant nothing to him but it was one of four that had been murdered earlier by that bitch that made this personal. She'd killed his brother. The kid was only nineteen. No one deserved to die the way she'd ended his life. Oh, he had plans for her. He was going to make her suffer. She would beg for death before he put the final nail in the coffin.

"We've got everyone out there searching for them as we speak," Joel said.

Joel Gonzales had been a good friend of his brother. He'd also taken the news of his brother's death hard but that didn't excuse a lapse in judgment.

"I want them found. Block off all the exit roads from Saranac."

"Already done, Dallas."

"Good." He nodded and approached the bar, scooping up a beer and cracking the top off. "Take four of the horses and leave only two men here. I want everyone searching homes, apartments, stores. You stick together in groups of twos."

"You want them dead or alive?"

"I want her alive. The rest you can kill."

Joel motioned with his head to the others and they left him alone sipping on beer. He sat at the counter staring into the mirror behind the bar. His hair was shoulder length, and he had a thick beard. His clothes were nothing more than dirty rags. He could barely recognize the man before him. It was a stark contrast. Before the EMP his world had been numbers and spreadsheets. He'd run a successful accounting business on the east side of Saranac. He wore high-end clothes, leased his vehicles and was careful about the company he kept. His business catered to large companies and corporations, those who had deep pockets and weren't afraid to spend. He had his hands in the real estate market and owned four apartment blocks in the town. Since the day he'd got into business, he'd had his eyes on retiring by the time he was fifty, and then living off passive income from his rentals and investments. Everything was working like clockwork. When he wasn't working or prowling cocktail bars for skirt, he'd research ways to increase his wealth through different forms of investments. He funneled money into his 401k, IRA, short-term bonds, fixed-income funds and had hired one of the best investments managers in the state. By all accounts he was living the American Dream.

His jaw clenched at how foolish he'd been.

For all the advice that he'd got to squirrel his money away, he hadn't thought about what would happen if the bottom dropped out. Now he had nothing, not even the gold he'd acquired was of use to him. Sure he could trade it but what use was that to anyone else? It was fucking pointless. He'd lived his life like a rat on a wheel, running fast, boasting about how much money he'd made and what a lavish lifestyle he led — for what? To be sitting in a dingy bar glancing at himself in a mirror. His parents were dead. His only brother was dead. He pulled the Sig Sauer from his holster and laid it in front of him. He had a good mind to end it right there and then. Even if he did catch this woman and punished her — what then? They were living on borrowed time. The whole damn country was. It was getting more dangerous out there by the day and even though his group offered protection, they couldn't provide medical care, food, water, or the basics of life. When it came down to it, these were all that mattered now — that and... family.

He tipped his head back and heaved a heavy sigh, then picked up the handgun and brought it up to his mouth. He stuck it inside and for a few seconds contemplated pulling the trigger. *Just squeeze it, you pussy! All the pain will be over. No more worry. No more problems.*

Right then the bell above the door let out a shrill as Joel returned.

"Oh, um..."

Dallas withdrew the gun from his mouth and glanced at him.

"What is it?"

"Ah, nothing, I was just going to get the keys to the Jeep from you."

He fished into his pocket and tossed them. "And Joel. Don't you say a word to anyone."

"Of course not. Look, I know how you feel."

"No you don't. Now get out of here."

Joel backed out closing the door behind him.

* * *

Back in Texas, under the cover of night, Ryan Hayes extracted the knife from the throat of one of the militia. He'd killed another three that evening right underneath their noses and he had no plans to stop. By the time morning came, Shelby would be bouncing off the walls in anger. He had no sympathy for these men. Some were probably good guys who just got suckered into Shelby's three percenters jargon. Freedom. The American Way. Beat your chest and sleep with your gun type of bullshit. It was all egotistical crap spewed from the mouths of guys who hadn't grown up. They were hypocrites. Did they think of America when they fired rounds into his father? No. All they cared about was getting inside these walls and controlling the masses. It was all smoke and mirrors. Even as he watched the new influx of refugees, he knew what kind of game Shelby was playing. He was leading them by the nose with promises of a new tomorrow. A land filled with milk and honey. Soon he would start spewing scriptures and demanding everyone to lend an ear and gather around. In his mind he was no different than David Koresh. A lunatic bent on brainwashing everyone and creating a cult following who would drop and give him twenty whenever he liked.

Well, it wasn't going to happen, at least not if he had any say in the matter. Ryan was going to be the fly in the ointment and make him regret ever killing his father. As he stepped back from the guy he'd dragged into the shadows just outside the athletic facilities, a military air raid siren screamed loudly. Harlan had obtained several prior to closing the gates in anticipation of an attack. It hadn't been much use the night Shelby showed up. Now its ear-piercing scream rang out as floodlights lit up the grounds. Panic rose in his chest. Ryan slipped the knife back into its sheath and tried to return without being seen. Already he could see Shelby's men driving everyone out of the bunkers. Over the sound of a loud megaphone, Shelby bellowed.

"You have five minutes to get outside now!"

He hadn't anticipated this.

Ryan hurried around trees hoping to make it to the phase 1 bunkers. That was not where his room was. Even if he made it inside without being seen, he would still have to crawl back through the vents to the phase 3 bunkers and then wipe off the camo face paint. He crouched down watching people running, some of the women were crying as the militia manhandled them. Then he spotted his moment to make a break for it. Hurrying back to the bunker he slipped inside and located one of the vents, he yanked it off and crawled inside. Sweat trickled down his face in the humid heat. On his hands and knees he scrambled through the steel maze, his heart racing, knowing full well he wasn't going to make it back in time.

By the time he reached his room, the door was already open. Soldiers had been in to find him. *Shit!* The jig was up. They would soon know it was him and he couldn't even lie and say he was sleeping. Ryan pushed out the vent and dropped down quietly. He could still hear the faint sound of Shelby bellowing outside. Moving at breakneck speed he pulled out the wipes and removed the thick wad of camo paint, then dropped it into a bag. He removed the dark clothing and stashed it above one of the ceiling tiles. Now only wearing a shirt, pants and socks, he hurried out into the empty corridor and made his way outside.

By the time he emerged everyone was on their knees with their hands behind their heads. Rifles were pointed at them and Shelby stood with his arms crossed. Ryan tried to act casual, but all eyes were on him. He joined the end of the line and dropped to his knees. Shelby eyed him suspiciously. *Any second now,* he thought. *He's going to come over and fire a round into my skull.* At least he'd managed to kill five of his men. He glanced down the line searching for his brother Sam. He wasn't there. Ryan frowned, then he spotted him in the next line. He breathed a sigh of relief.

"Someone was out tonight killing more of my men," Shelby began. "Now, I've been more than lenient but tonight it ends." He paced back and forth, his eyes washing over everyone. Several of the women sobbed quietly. "Don't you get it? We are trying to help you all. Had we not arrived some other group would have entered and killed you all. We didn't kill you, and we have been nothing but good toward you."

"That's bullshit," someone said. Ryan looked down the line and watched as Shelby's brother pulled Timothy Heart out of the group. His wife tried to stop them but was struck in the face with a rifle. That caused even more outrage, but it soon ended as Shelby's men rushed in and started beating people with batons. It was like watching the beginning of a riot, except these people weren't rioting; Tim's closest friends were just trying to protect him.

Tim was dragged in front of Shelby and tossed on his knees.

Shelby crouched down and cupped a hand over his ear.

"You want to run that by me again?"

"I said this is bullshit. You killed our people."

"Your people?" He laughed and looked over to Harlan. "Seems you really were doing a shit job of leading these folks. Who else wants to act like they're in charge?" His eyes darted to Ryan before looking back at Tim.

"You people really are as dumb as you look. You bought into Harlan's spiel hook, line and sinker not realizing that it doesn't matter if you hide behind walls — your defense is only good as those guarding it. You did a shit job of protecting this property when we arrived. We proved that. Now we could have killed all of you but we didn't." He paused to gather his thoughts. "Yes, we killed some of you."

"What?" a woman piped up. She was new to the

compound. And by the expressions on the faces of those who'd arrived that evening, they hadn't been made aware of this.

"It has no bearing on your survival here." Shelby rose to his feet. "You came to us willingly. We opened our doors. None of you had to enter. And since arriving, have we not given you a warm bed, warm food? And have you not appreciated the security that my men provide?"

He waited for an answer but no one replied.

Shelby turned his attention back to Timothy.

"So yes, we killed some of you in order to show you how weak this chain really was. If we hadn't done it, someone else would have and perhaps they wouldn't have been so forgiving. Now I have tried to work with you, but you are forcing my hand. I have given you multiple chances to give up the one responsible for killing my men, and how do you repay me? By killing more." He paused. "Well it ends tonight!"

"Just kill me and get it over with, I'm growing tired of listening to your shit!" Timothy said. Shelby walked over and crouched down.

"Oh, I'm not going to kill you. No, you've already done that to yourself. But you are going to suffer. There will be different levels of suffering, depending on the gravity of your crimes." He turned to his brother. "Take him to the sweatbox."

"What?" Tim asked. Two hulking men grabbed an arm and dragged Tim away as his wife protested. Ryan wasn't aware of any sweatboxes. They were often used out in the Middle East as an extreme form of solitary confinement and torture. Using the humidity of arid regions, the sweatbox would dehydrate a person, cause heat exhaustion and even lead to death depending on how long someone was kept inside.

"Now let this be seen as a lesson to you all. I am for you. I will fight for you. But I will not be taken for a fool. You are not slaves, and I'm not here to mother you. If you can't understand what we are trying to build, then leave now! But for those of you who choose to remain, be assured that punishment does exist and we will act swiftly."

"What did he do?" his wife, Sharon, cried out.

Without missing a beat, Shelby replied, "He bit the hand that fed him."

She broke down and was led away by another soldier. Meanwhile a few people from the recent arrivals got up and headed for the gates. Ryan fully expected Shelby to kill them but he didn't. There was a reason why he was letting them walk, and a reason why he was punishing Timothy. He wanted everyone to know he was a man of his word, and yet fair at the same time. This was control at its finest. Other than the twelve people who opted to leave the compound that night, the rest remained.

Chapter 15

As soon as Maggie fixed the flashlight on Rayna, she knew something had gone horribly wrong. Her eyes were swollen from crying, she had a cut lip and bruising to the side of her face. *Who was this new person with her? Where was Jill?*

"Jesse, Rayna's back!"

She hurried over to meet her and the first words out of her mouth were, "Where's Jill?" Right then Rayna burst out crying and collapsed into her arms. She hugged her tight and eyed the girl behind her who looked nervous.

"Rayna?" Jesse said jogging over. "What happened?"

She could barely get words out. "Where's Elliot?"

"In trouble," Jesse replied. "You weren't here when we got the call. I've been trying his radio since but can't get through." He looked at the girl beside her. "Who's this?"

"I'm Brianna," she said extending her hand. Jesse just stared so Maggie leaned forward and shook it.

Rayna made a gesture. "Maggie, can you show Brianna to the bunker while I go take a bath?"

"Sure. What about your kids?"

"Where are they?"

"In the bunker."

"Don't tell them I'm here yet."

That struck her as odd. She absolutely adored her kids. As she broke away and headed for Mr. Thompson's house, Maggie noticed the way she was walking like she was in pain. Maggie turned to Brianna.

"You want to fill in the blanks?"

The girl nodded and began to outline all that had led to her meeting Rayna. Twenty minutes later, Maggie cut Jesse a glance. She couldn't fathom that Jill was dead or that Rayna had been raped and forced to take drugs. They gave Brianna some food and water and led her to a bed where she could rest while they went outside and spoke with the others about what to do. It was like their group was coming apart at the seams. Even if they could reach Elliot, what would they tell him?

Twenty minutes later, Jesse took a seat on a log around the campfire. He stirred up the flames with a metal rod that once was a coat hanger. There was silence for a few minutes between them as they came to grips with all that had happened.

He ran a hand over his head. "Even if he makes it back. He won't have anyone to go after. She's already killed him."

Maggie nodded. "This is going to change everything."

"You think?" Jesse said sarcastically.

She would have called him out on it but lately everyone had been on edge. Months of trying to survive had worn away at their tough exterior. It had beaten them down, changed them. Some became harder and wiser, others jaded, and the rest had been left shell-shocked. She'd seen the way the neighbors along the street had reacted after the final collapse of infrastructure. Some retreated into their homes, others lobbied for Gary to oversee them, while the rest took it upon themselves to roll up their sleeves and step up. It was a mixed bag because that's what people were. No one viewed the world the same. That irritated some folks and made others smile.

"We need to head to Saranac," Jesse said.

"Yeah? And how are we going to get there?"

"How did we get here?"

She scoffed. "I'm not riding a bike."

"Then do you have a better idea?" He paused. "It will only take an hour to get there by bike."

"And when do you want to leave?"

"At dawn."

"By then they could be dead."

"You don't know that. Anyway, we're of no use to them tired. We have to hope they can handle themselves in the meantime. We should get some rest."

She stared at him. "You want to take others with us?"

"Only those that will go." Jesse sighed. "They should have been back by now, Maggie. And you know Elliot. He wouldn't have got on that radio and caused Rayna any unnecessary worry if he thought they could handle it.

Whatever shit they've got themselves into, they need our help."

She blew out her cheeks and leaned forward stretching. Jesse got up and came around the back of her. He placed his hands on her shoulders and began rubbing them. They'd grown close over the past six months, but it hadn't turned into anything serious. It was hard to experience any deep level of intimacy while the world was falling down around them. She moaned a little as his fingers worked into her joints and eased the tension.

"I should probably go and be with Rayna. Maybe you can keep an eye on Brianna."

He released his grip and nodded.

If she was being honest, she just wasn't ready for anything more than friendship. After all she'd been through with her loser of a boyfriend in New York, the thought of being treated right seemed like a joke. Her walls were still up, and she wasn't sure if that would change.

* * *

Back in Saranac, Elliot and the others had ventured out determined to not leave without at least the Jeep, or a couple of horses. Instead of just walking the streets they opted to find high ground and assess the situation.

"We don't know how many are out there," Elliot said.

"And you expect to find out by standing up here?" Gary asked. "Let's just go home, Elliot. Leave now while we still have our lives."

"Not until we get transportation."

"I will not have you play roulette with my life."

"Then leave. No one is holding you here, Gary. You want to go, go!" Elliot said. "And that goes for the rest of you."

Gary snorted. "You get off on this, don't you?"

Elliot turned. "What?"

"This. Being out here, knee deep in the grime. I bet if you hadn't been given that medical discharge you would have taken another tour, wouldn't you?"

Elliot didn't reply.

"Admit it. You're addicted to war. If you're not in it,

you're creating it."

"Why don't you give him a break?" Damon said from across the other side of the building. They were standing on top of DJ's Rustic Restaurant just off Broadway Street. They didn't pick it because it offered the best scope of the land but because Sean had spotted an armed group of about ten heading their way.

"Why don't you shut the fuck up?" Gary replied.

"Make me."

"Oh please!" Ella shook her head. "Are you guys always like this? At each other's throats? It must be a real joy to be around you all."

"Well if you don't like it," Sean said, "I'd gladly hand you over to that lunatic. At least then we might be able to leave."

"Try it," she said squaring up to him. Elliot chuckled. That girl had large kahooners. She reminded him of Rayna.

"You know I really could go for a large Big Mac about now," Zach said without looking at anyone. He was crouched down picking at the metal air vent on the roof of the restaurant. "You think they might have something inside?"

The very thought of food made Elliot's stomach grumble. They hadn't eaten in hours. But it wasn't food he was worried about, it was thirst. He could kill for a bottle of water.

"Why don't you go and take a look?" Gary said. "As it seems we are going to be here all night," he added while glaring at Elliot. Elliot understood why Gary wanted to leave, that's why he didn't take offense to his off-the-cuff remarks and griping. If he had his own way, he would be at home, inside the bunker curled up with Rayna, but going back empty-handed, hell, going back with even less than they set out with, wasn't in the cards. Despite what Gary believed, Elliot didn't get a hardon over war, or facing off against any of these lunatics. It was a matter of principle. The day was not going to waste if he had his way. He pulled the magazine from his rifle to check how many rounds he had left. *Eight.* Gary and Damon were both out, and finding ammo, more specifically ammo for these AR-15s, wasn't going to be easy. No, the only way forward now was to attack a smaller group and use their weapons.

"Get down!" he said. Everyone dropped. The sound of voices could be heard long before he saw them. Elliot crawled to the far corner of the building and peered over. Heading south on Broadway was a group of four. All of them were armed and the chance of them being able to take them out with eight bullets was slim.

"What have we got?" Gary asked sliding up beside him.

"Four. I can probably take out two before the others turn and fire but it would be taking a risk."

"Then don't."

"If we don't get our hands on some loaded firearms we aren't getting out of here, Gary."

"We have made it this far, and we have Ella. She's avoided them for two months. This is a simple case of you not wanting to leave."

Elliot chuckled. "No, this is a case of me not listening to you. It burns you to know that I was right about Lake Placid. I told you it was going to collapse, that people would only hold their positions for a few weeks at most but you refused to believe it. You held out hope until the end."

"And that's wrong?" he shot back.

"No. But you're still thinking with the same mindset. Run instead of fight. Avoid instead of confront."

"Maybe. But that's what's kept us alive."

Elliot shook his head and returned to looking over the edge. They were much closer now. In a matter of minutes they would be directly below and passing them. He planned on shooting two of them from behind. Best case scenario, the other two would flee, worst case, they would fire back and others would arrive to provide backup. There was no easy way of doing this. No guarantee in this new world. Every decision made, every action could backfire. It didn't matter how much training people had. How tactically sound they thought they were. Shit could go south real quick.

Elliot whistled over to Damon and motioned with his head. He crossed over keeping low to the roof.

"What do you want?"

"I'm taking two of them out. We need to grab those weapons fast. You up for it?"

He shrugged. "What's option two?"

"There isn't one."

"I thought so. Yeah. I'll head down with Sean. If things get hot, I'll use him as a shield," he said before chuckling. Sean glared at him.

"I'm not going down."

"Then I'll take Zach."

"Fuck that," Zach replied.

"Oh for goodness' sakes, I'll go with you," Ella said, crossing over to the rear of the building and using the drainpipe to climb down.

"Hurry, Damon," Elliot said noticing the men were getting closer. He kept watch on the group and prepared to take the shot.

He could hear them talking among themselves.

"I just don't see what all the fuss is about. So they escaped. Let them go."

"You heard Dallas. He wants her."

"Because he lost his brother? Boo fucking hoo. We've all lost family."

"Yeah, well you say that to his face."

They strolled past and Elliot brought his rifle up and fixed his crosshair on the back of the nearest guy's head. He slowed his breathing and then took the shot. Quickly he adjusted, shifting to the next guy as they registered they were under attack. Another crack and the guy beside him hit the pavement. The other spun around but couldn't get a bead on where the shots originated. Elliot used that to his advantage as they backed up fast. One more round punctured a guy's noggin, knocking him to the ground. The fourth guy took off, sprinting. Elliot fired again and caught him in the leg. He buckled and landed hard, his gun flying out of his hands. He'd only made it about ten yards when Damon and Ella burst out of the shadows to scoop up the weapons. Elliot homed in on the guy who was groaning in agony and crawling on his belly trying to make it to his weapon. He didn't stand a chance. A slow-moving target was too easy. Another round echoed, and it was done but far from over. The sound of gunfire would attract more. One group was never that far from another. Elliot had to take his hat off to Dallas; he sure knew how to rally the troops. If they could have only had a man like that on their side, perhaps they would have been able to hold back the flood of raiders that Lake Placid was experiencing.

Ella scooped up the rifles, and they hurried back. While they were doing that another group of four were making their way down. They needed to shift position and fast. Anywhere was better than here.

"Go. Go!" Gary yelled as Ella returned and handed over rifles and magazines. They juggled them in their hands while heading up Prospect Drive. Elliot planned on swinging around and approaching the bar from the rear. He figured they would expect them to stay clear of the place and most if not all of Dallas's men would be out searching for them. They decided to cut through the backyards of homes on McComb Street and head for Terrace Street which butted up against the back of the bar.

They could already hear yelling.

"Sounds like they've found their dead pals," Gary said.

"Stay alert, folks," Elliot added as they darted from one tree to the next, keeping in the shadows.

"I swear if even one of us dies, you and are I are going to have issues," Gary said in a threatening manner. He'd forgotten that Elliot had told him he didn't have to stay. The fact was he knew they stood a better chance sticking together than going it alone. As they got closer to the bar, Elliot's heart slammed against his chest. His brow was covered in sweat. A flashback from his time in Iraq hit him. The sound of gunfire. Bombs going off. Flames and one of his men yelling for help.

He pushed the past from his mind. He had to stay focused.

Not now. Not now! He told himself.

As they got closer to the rear of the bar, they dropped down behind trees and assessed the situation. There was no one outside. There were a few horses tied up but no Jeep.

"There we go. We take those and get out of here," Gary said.

"And the Jeep?"

"Don't push it, Elliot!"

He nodded, and they moved in.

Chapter 16

Ryan trudged back to his room with the rest of the group. They dispersed once inside the bunkers, each heading off down the tunnels to their allocated abode. Upon entering his room he found his brother Samuel sitting on a chair holding a tub of camo paint and eyeing him.

"Where did you find that?" Ryan asked.

He jerked his head toward the door. "Close the door."

Ryan pushed it shut and his brother rose. "You want to tell me why you lied to me?"

"I don't know what you're talking about."

"Ryan, don't bullshit me. It was you." He stooped and reached under the bed and pulled out the gear Ryan had been wearing. Ryan frowned then hopped up onto the bed and pushed up the ceiling tile.

"Don't bother. It's all here."

"How did you know?"

"Besides that fact that you're the only one in this compound who'd have the balls to do it? Um, maybe because we think alike. There are only so many places you could have hidden a knife. Do you really think they wouldn't have found this? You would have been better off leaving it somewhere inside the air vent or buried." He tossed it at him. "You need to get rid of that and fast."

"They haven't figured it out yet."

"No, but they are planning on performing a search of the rooms."

Ryan shifted his weight from one foot to the next. "How do you know that?"

"I overhead John Shelby talking with his brother." Samuel stared back at him, squinting. "Oh hold on, you thought when they dragged Tim to the sweatbox that it was going to suffice for the killings tonight? Please." He shook his head. "That was just the beginning. Nothing more than a spectacle."

"I know what I'm doing," Ryan said.

"Dad would have gone berserk if he was here, and you

know that."

"If he was here, I wouldn't be doing it."

"Yes you would."

Ryan took the clothing, knife and camo paint and climbed back up to hide it behind the ceiling tile. "Listen, little brother, we are going to be fine."

"Don't be condescending and speak down to me. You are playing with fire, Ryan, and maybe you've managed to get away with it so far but eventually your luck is going to run out. You think he's going to let you keep killing his men every night?"

"He has so far."

Samuel shook his head and looked at the ground. "Do you care so little about your life that you are willing to risk it just to take back this place from one man, only to hand it over to another?"

"What are you on about?" Ryan asked.

"You heard him. I might not agree with Shelby but he was right. He could have killed all of us when they raided this place. Someone else might not have been as lenient."

Ryan leaned toward him. "Lenient? Have you forgotten that man killed our father?"

"No. But he knew the risk just as we do. And Shelby might have a god complex, and he might be following some skewed ideology, but he's still feeding us, we are still sheltered and come to think if it, we are protected."

"Protected? These men aren't going to protect you. They are protecting themselves and acting as if they are doing us a favor. We are simply a means to an end. Once he has earned the trust of people in here and believe me, he will, he'll change the rules."

"I don't like it, Ryan, any more than you do but unless you're willing to walk out those gates and leave this place behind, then we need to abide by their rules."

"Listen to yourself. He's already inside your head." Ryan tapped his brother's temple with a finger. "The only reason he let those twelve walk out the gate was to manipulate people into believing that he's a fair man. He wants to give a false sense of security. Now if all of us were to try and walk out, you can be sure he would stop it."

"You don't know that."

"Well then try it," Ryan shot back.

"I don't want to leave."

Ryan snorted and shook his head.

Samuel continued, "No, I'm serious. It's bad out there, Ryan. At least here we are behind walls, inside bunkers and have enough food for the next three years. So he has a few rules. So did Harlan."

"Yeah but Harlan isn't a sociopath."

"No, he's a coward," Samuel replied.

Ryan stared at him with an expression of confusion. "If you're not doing anything about it, then so are you."

"I would but it's just…" he trailed off.

"It's what? Sam. C'mon. Work with me, brother, to take them down from the inside."

He dipped his head. "I'm sorry. I can't."

"You can't or you won't?"

"Both." Samuel turned towards the door.

"Then where does that leave you and me?"

"What do you mean?" Samuel asked.

"You are either for or against him. And if you're for him — you want his men to live."

"And?"

"So are you going to say anything?" Ryan asked.

"I wouldn't do that."

"No? Because it sounds an awful lot like you are against me."

Samuel turned back. "That's because I give a shit about whether you live or die, Ryan. You're my only kin. Do you think I want you dead?" His gaze penetrated him. "If I could change this situation, I would but killing them is only going to heap hot coals on everyone's head. You are causing all of us to suffer. Now I'm asking you as your brother. Stop. Don't kill anyone else."

"I can't do that."

Sam clenched his jaw and looked away from him. Without saying any more he walked out and slammed the door behind him. Ryan let out a heavy sigh and slumped down on his bed.

* * *

Elliot and the others had been observing the Rusty Nail for the better part of twenty minutes after moving in a little closer. Something about it didn't feel right. Two horses tied up outside in the open with no one guarding them? He placed a hand on Gary's chest just as Gary was about to head out with Sean and Zach. They were going to collect the horses while he, Damon and Ella provided cover.

"Wait!"

"For what?" Gary asked.

"Where is everyone?"

"Searching for us. We need to do this now, Elliot."

"No, something's not right."

"The only thing that isn't right is staying a minute longer in this shithole of a town. Now I'm going in with or without you."

This was unlike Gary. He was used to planning everything out methodically. If there was even a hint of risk involved he'd overanalyze it, now he was just functioning on pure emotion.

He motioned to Sean and Zach and they darted out of the tree line, pitching sideways down a rocky slope behind the garage area before hopping down off a seven-foot wall to the ground. Elliot had to run with it. He motioned for Damon and Ella to provide cover from the east and west while Elliot came down the middle and made sure that if anyone dashed out of the garage or bar, he could take them out.

Their actions were fast, purposeful and quiet but what they hadn't noticed was a sniper on the far side of the road perched inside a house directly across from the bar. It was only when a crack echoed and Sean collapsed that all hell broke loose. The two horses reared up, frightened, and tugged on the rope holding them to the garage.

"Gary!" Elliot shouted hurrying down, while he was still trying to get a bead on where the shooter was. Gary was determined to get one of those horses, regardless of how many shooters there were. More gunfire erupted, this time coming from Damon, then it was Ella.

"They're coming. We got to move!" Damon said.

Right then Dallas came out of the bar. Everything was happening so fast. Zach was firing back when Dallas appeared behind him, raised his gun and fired a round into his skull. He didn't stand a chance.

By now Gary was up on a horse. But the horse was too overwhelmed by the noise of gunfire. It reared back knocking him off. He landed hard and as Elliot rushed to get him he came under fire from Dallas. There was no way in hell he was going to let him take Gary. Elliot pressed forward, blocking out his fear that was telling him to run. He unloaded round after round forcing Dallas to take cover inside the bar. Not even for a second did he let up squeezing the trigger. Gary was on the ground, groaning and holding his head. When he landed, his back had taken the full brunt of the fall and he'd smacked his head on the concrete.

"Get up now!" Elliot said, squeezing off rounds up at the shooter in the window across the road. He scooped an arm under Gary's and pulled him to his feet while continuing to engage. They stumbled back, and he nearly lost his footing. He cried out for help from Damon but both he and Ella were holding back the new influx of fighters. Ella rushed back passing by the bar. She didn't see Dallas emerge. He blindsided her by tackling her to the ground. There was no time to help her. Elliot, Gary and Damon retreated up the road, passed the wall and climbed up a grassy embankment before disappearing into the dense trees. Gary was hurt bad.

"I think I've broken ribs." His breathing was shallow, and he was wincing in pain every few seconds as they picked up their pace and weaved in and out of trees and broke out onto Alpine Trail. Behind them they could hear Dallas yelling for his men to pursue them. Homes blurred in Elliot's peripheral vision as he stayed fixed on the road ahead. They veered down Neil Street, then crossed William, and slipped through the backyards of many of the homes. The only thing they had going for them was the area had a lot of trees and it was dark, making it easier for them to escape.

They kept running, putting distance between themselves and the bar until they made it to School Street. Elliot burst through a thicket of trees into the backyard of a home and tried the doors. Four homes later, they found one that was unlocked. They slipped inside and crouched down as Dallas's group combed through the streets hunting them.

* * *

At the same time that evening, as Ryan prepared to turn in for the night, a commotion could be heard out in the hallway. He ignored it thinking it was just the militia coming down heavy on a few of the residents. That soon changed when he heard Shelby's voice echo over the megaphone.

"Everyone outside your rooms, right now!"

He bounced off the bed, glanced up at the ceiling and contemplated removing the outfit and hiding it inside the vent, but before he had a chance to get up there, the door swung open and a soldier pointed.

"Didn't you hear? Outside now!"

He swallowed hard and stepped out. The soldier pressed him against the wall and moved on to the next room. Up and down the hallway, soldiers were going in and out, tearing the rooms apart. Frank Shelby came into view, a smile dancing on his face.

"This won't take long. Unfortunately due to this evening's incident, and to ensure the safety of all residents, we have to perform a routine search. If you have nothing to hide, there will be no problem."

Farther down the hall a soldier appeared holding a Glock. He handed it over to Shelby and then pointed to Steve Colson, a resident six doors down from Ryan — a good guy, a family man who had once been the supervisor for a house building company. He'd been one of the many involved in the construction of New Hope Springs.

Shelby walked up to him. "This belong to you?"

He nodded.

"Now I'm pretty sure I made it clear that all weapons were to be handed over until we could determine no one would be a threat. You want to explain how this didn't find its way into the hands of my men?"

Colson looked at the ground.

"Take him away, put him in the sweatbox."

A soldier grabbed him and hauled him off as his wife protested.

"That goes for all of you. I will not tolerate insubordination. A small leak is all it takes for a ship to sink. For those of you here who think I'm being too harsh, let me remind you that what we are doing here is for your benefit as well as ours."

Two soldiers entered Ryan's room and turned over the mattress, pulled out his drawers and tossed everything onto the ground. Then one stepped up onto the bedframe and began lifting ceiling tiles. He hadn't seen him do that in the room across from him. Why was he doing it here? Ryan glanced toward his brother who was standing outside his room with his chin dropped.

"What do we have here?" the soldier said pulling out his dark outfit and the knife. The soldier grinned as he walked past him and held it in the air. "We have a winner!"

Shelby strode the hallway, a glint of amusement in his expression.

"Well done," he said, taking the knife from him and looking at the blade which was still covered in dry blood. His eyes met Ryan's. Shelby shook his head and made a tutting sound. "Oh this is going to be a very bad night for you. And to think I placed my trust in you, Ryan. Well, do you have anything to say?"

"Yeah. Fuck you!"

"Take him away."

"To the sweatbox?" the soldier asked.

"No, I have something better planned for him."

Ryan struggled in their grip as two of them strong-armed him down the hallway and out of the bunker.

* * *

When he was gone, Frank ordered everyone back into their rooms. As doors closed, he made his way down to Samuel Hayes. He knocked on the door and entered, then shut the door behind him. He was still holding

Ryan's belongings.

"What you told me earlier has not gone unnoticed. I respect your honesty and it pleases me to know that we are finally getting through to some of you."

"What are you going to do with him?" Samuel asked.

"I haven't quite decided yet but I have to set an example. You know, so others won't pick up the baton after him."

"You said you'd be fair."

"And I will. You have my word on that. However, he's killed five of my men. That can't be allowed to happen again. Now, I wanted to discuss something else with you. A vacancy has just opened up and I think you have proven you can do the job."

"Which is?" Samuel asked.

"Observe, keep your ears to the ground and let me know if anyone is trying to go against me." He paused. "Do you want the job?"

He looked hesitant for a second then nodded.

"Good." He laid a hand on Samuel's shoulder.

"Tonight, you have earned my trust. You've done what no one else was able or willing to do. And the fact that he's your brother only confirms you are the right person."

"You won't tell him, will you?"

His lip twisted. "Of course not. No, this is between you and me."

Chapter 17

Mr. Thompson's home backed up to a small river. It was one several sources of water they used for cleaning and bathing. Most of the time they would just bathe in the river itself but when they had time, they would lug back buckets and boil the water so they could have a warm bath every couple of weeks. It was a treat. However, that evening Rayna didn't bother. She'd stripped off and slipped down into the cool waters, her mind didn't focus on how cold it was as she was too busy thinking about Jill and the attack on her body by Doc. Fragments of what he'd done to her came back through the hazy fog caused by the drugs. Most of all, she recalled feeling helpless. Zip tied, her only means of fighting him off was with her legs, and after being slapped around the face, and having a needle stuck in her, she soon became compliant. In many ways she was glad he'd drugged her. She didn't want to remember what he'd done. The few slivers of what she could make out made her want to vomit.

Rayna scrubbed herself clean, tears running down her face.

It felt like someone had shattered her innermost being.

The part of her that was strong was still there but battered and bruised. It would take some time to regain her self-confidence. Even then as she washed herself, her eyes roamed the trees expecting someone to attack. She hadn't felt that way before. Well not exactly. Of course, she knew how dangerous it was but she just didn't think she would become a victim. As for Jill? Her mind drifted to the past. It wasn't just the loss of her friend that pained her; it was the fact that she'd led her into it. *Why didn't you run, Jill?* She wondered. *Why didn't you just return and get help?* It was like she had something to prove. Maybe she did.

"Rayna," Maggie said, her voice startling her. She clutched her breasts with both arms and stood there feeling even more exposed than ever. "I just wanted to check in on you and see if there was anything I could do?"

She nodded, then shook her head. "Are my kids okay?"

"Yeah, they're sleeping."

"And Brianna?"

"Resting."

Maggie looked at the towel hanging on a tree branch.

"Could you?" Rayna asked motioning to the towel.

"Yeah, sure."

Maggie handed it to her, and she slipped out of the water and wrapped herself. Rayna could tell by the way Maggie was looking at her bruises that she was full of questions.

"She told you, didn't she?"

Maggie nodded. "I'm so sorry, Rayna."

She shrugged as they made their way back to the house. "There's nothing you could have done."

"What happened?"

She sighed, wanting to cry again but felt too numb. Instead she brought her up to speed on everything that had led to her capture by Doc, and what she'd seen when she came to. They entered Mr. Thompson's home and

Maggie handed her a set of clothes that she had brought over.

"I thought you would need these."

She offered back a faint smile. "Right, I appreciate it."

Rayna took them and spent a minute getting changed.

"You going to come back to the bunker tonight?"

"No, I think I'm going to sleep here for the night."

Maggie got this surprised expression on her face. "Oh. Then I'll stay with you."

"You don't have to do that."

"But I want to."

"I can take care of myself."

"I know you can but…"

"Please. Maggie. I just want to be left alone."

She walked over to the liquor bar and pulled out a bottle of bourbon. She poured it neat and tossed it back like water. It burned her throat. A few more and she wouldn't remember what had happened, at least until the morning.

"Okay, I'll sleep outside. It's a warm night."

That made Rayna smile a little.

"You're persistent."

She took a few steps forward. "I know you probably don't want to hear it and I'm not entirely sure what went on but I want you to know that I understand what it feels like."

"Do you?" Rayna said in a hard tone.

Silence stretched between them.

"The first time he raped me was one year into our relationship," she said. Rayna looked at her through confused eyes. "My boyfriend back in New York. Before he lashed out, he took advantage of me."

Rayna frowned.

"I said no, but he did it anyway."

"Did you ever tell anyone?" she asked.

"Who would have believed me? We were in a relationship. He would have said it was consensual. I didn't know anyone in New York except a couple of people whereas he'd lived there his whole life. His parents had connections. And he had been drinking that night. I just notched it up to the alcohol. I mean he'd never done it before." She took a deep breath while Rayna lit a couple of candles. "The second and last time he did it was the week we broke up. I went to the police and got a restraining order put on him."

"Did you tell them?"

She shook her head.

"Did you go to the hospital to get examined?"

"No point. It wasn't…" She sighed. "How do I put this? He wasn't aggressive enough to leave bruising or anything that would have given a doctor reason to believe that I had been assaulted. He simply continued when I told him no. Unfortunately there are a lot of women out there who have been in the same position. They're dating, they don't want to offend or lose their partner, or they don't know where the line in the sand is drawn."

"It's drawn at no," Rayna said.

She nodded. "Yeah, I understand that now. That's why I left him. Besides the fact that he was an asshole and had backhanded me numerous times."

Maggie had caring eyes and Rayna could tell she understood on some level. Obviously it wasn't the same situation but the non-consensual act was still the same.

"Thank you, Maggie," she said in a quiet voice.

"For what?"

"For being here. Coming to Lake Placid."

Maggie returned a warm smile and for a brief moment, Rayna felt hope, even if it was only a sliver.

"I'm going to turn in for the night," Rayna said.

"Okay. Um, we're going to leave at dawn for Saranac."

"Elliot. Right." She nodded but couldn't see her way to express more than that. She had to believe that whatever situation Elliot and the others were in, they would get themselves out of it. She trusted his skillset and with both Gary and Elliot working together, she felt confident there was no challenge they couldn't overcome.

* * *

Damon used the cigarette lighter to illuminate the inside of the home. There before him was a couple slumped against each other, or at least what was left of them. The smell of rotting flesh was something no one got used to. Back in the bunker he had a small tub of Vicks that he'd usually take out with him when they went scavenging. He'd smear a few fingers' worth below his nose and that had always done the trick. He'd forgotten to bring it with him this time.

"Looks like he killed his wife and shot himself. Poor bastards," Damon said.

Over the past six months, life hadn't just become hard physically but emotionally. Everywhere they turned there was something trying to dim the flicker of hope inside them. If people weren't being murdered, they were committing suicide because it was easier than trying to make it through another day. Often he would find himself chuckling as he thought about all the people that used to complain about how hard life was. Before the lights went out, life was a walk in the park. Sure, it was full of stress and could throw a curve ball once in a while but it was nothing compared to now.

"Put that light out," Elliot said. He turned his

attention to Gary who had one hand on his back and the other on his head. He was groaning.

"Go on, say it," Gary said through gritted teeth. "Go on. I told you so. That's what you're going to say, isn't it, Elliot?"

"Shut up, Gary. God, you go on like an old woman."

Elliot stood by the window glancing out, hoping that trouble didn't come their way.

"We'll wait until the early hours of the morning and go get her," Damon said.

"We're not going back, Damon," Elliot responded. "At the first chance we get, we are leaving this town."

"What happened to, we need to get a vehicle? A horse?"

"That was before I realized how many people Dallas has in his group. There are too many of them out there. We are lucky to still be alive."

"I'm not leaving Ella with him. You know what he will do."

"She's not our problem."

"That problem is the reason why we are still alive. She navigated us through these streets, without her we'll be lucky to make it five blocks without getting shot. And anyway, if we leave now, how are we going to get to this compound in Texas?"

"The same way we got from New York to Lake Placid. Through pure determination."

"Bullshit."

Elliot looked at him as if he was about to comment but then returned to gazing out into the night. Damon glanced at his watch, it was close to midnight. A wave of tiredness hit him. They'd been up before the crack of dawn and spent the better part of the day on the run. He was hungry, thirsty, desperate for sleep, and worried for Ella. He didn't expect to get any support from either of them. They hadn't said a word about Sean or Zach since losing them back there. The fact was, all that mattered was staying alive. Once someone was dead, they were dead. Gone. It was a waste of energy to grieve for them.

"Well, I'm going to get her, with or without you."

"Then it will be without us, I'm afraid," Elliot replied. Gary didn't need to say anything, Damon already knew his answer. He wandered off into the kitchen to see what he could find in the cupboards to eat.

* * *

Under a full moon that night, Ryan's hands were handcuffed to a thick chain, and he was hoisted up against a large pole in the middle of the yard. His feet dangled, his toes barely touching the ground. Within minutes of hanging there he could already feel the strain on his ligaments. Blood trickled from his mouth, his eyes were swollen from where four of the militia had beaten him senseless. Retribution for killing their buddies, they said. Shelby didn't stop them. He wasn't even around when they did it. He passed out several times and when he did, they would urinate on him and continue the assault. They cracked his ribs with batons and took turns striking him in the jaw and beating his knees with plastic piping. They'd broken two teeth, and he was sure they'd ruptured blood vessels in his eyes. Out of the swollen slits of his eyes he could barely see. They'd even removed his shoes and used a metal pole to crush three of his toes. At some point he must have blacked out. All he felt now was pain, excruciating pain shooting from his feet to his head. Two more hard jabs to the stomach and he heard Shelby's voice.

"That's enough!"

In the darkness all he saw was his silhouette approaching.

He leaned forward, his lips inches away from Ryan's ear. "You know you brought this on yourself. You only have yourself to blame. However, there is a silver lining to every dark cloud. Would you like to know what it is?"

He didn't respond. Even if he could, he wouldn't have.

"The others will no longer be punished. They will get to eat. They will still work on the wall but they will eat. They have your brother to thank for that."

Ryan raised his head; his brow pinched causing him even more pain.

"Oh you didn't know? That's right." He let out a sigh.

"He made me promise that I wouldn't tell you. You know how it is with brothers. Loyalty and whatnot." He smiled. "Except his loyalty is with me now. He will be doing the job you should have done. Your brother is my eyes and ears now. And what a fine job he has done."

"You bastard," Ryan said through gritted teeth.

"Oh, come on, Ryan. Don't you have a sense of humor?" He took out a cigarette and lit it. Shelby blew smoke into his face. "From here on out it's all smooth sailing. You see, I'm not going to kill you, Ryan. I thought about it. Hell, my men would love to keep beating you until you give up the ghost but what would that accomplish? It would only turn you into a martyr. No, I'm going to keep you alive. Barely. But still, I'll keep you alive and let everyone inside this compound see what happens when they cross over the line." He looked at him without saying anything, and then added, "In fact I should be thanking you because you've just made my job easier."

Ryan muttered something.

"What's that?" Shelby asked leaning in closer.

"I'm going to kill you," Ryan said in a barely audible voice.

"Um. No. I didn't quite catch that. You are going to need to speak louder."

He got closer, close enough for Ryan to do the only thing he could — bite.

Ryan latched on to his ear and tore away.

Shelby let out a bloodcurdling scream and staggered back clutching what remained of his ear. What came next was more pain but it was worth it. In fact he laughed as they beat his body with batons and struck his face causing him to bleed even more. The last thing he recalled before blacking out was Shelby screaming and staggering away towards the bunkers.

Chapter 18

The sound of a door slamming stirred Elliot awake. He immediately put his hand on his rifle and sat up. He'd had trouble staying alert throughout the night. Gary wasn't able to help due to the pain in his back, which had only got worse as the night wore on. He scrambled to his feet and glanced at his watch. It was still early. Just after five. Outside he saw Damon crouched by a tree checking his rifle. Gary was still asleep. Elliot went out.

"C'mon, Damon, where are you heading?"

"Already told you. I'm going to get her."

He shook his head. "That's not a smart idea."

"Neither was going for those damn horses but I went with you."

Elliot pawed at his tired eyes and scanned the area for threats. "You know I would go but Gary's condition has got worse overnight. I need to get him home."

"That's fine. I need to get her."

"Why? You don't owe her anything. All right, sure, she helped us navigate the streets but she's not flesh and blood, and you damn sure aren't dating the chick."

"She has no one else, Elliot. Neither do I."

"You have us."

Damon stared intently before looking away. "It's the right thing to do."

"That doesn't make it the smart thing."

"Right. Smart. It doesn't matter. It's what I need to do."

Elliot wasn't going to continue arguing with him, when Damon made up his mind to do something he followed through. His return to Keene had been proof of that.

"You got enough ammo?"

He nodded. "Thanks to those four guys."

Elliot looked off into the distance as the sun's bright morning rays filtered through the trees. It was already beginning to warm up. He expected another hot day.

"Listen, when we get back, we are probably going to

leave for Texas within twenty-four hours. With all that's happened over the last month, and with what Ella knows about our place in Lake Placid, it's just not safe for us to remain there any longer. If you're not there tomorrow at six in the morning…"

"You'll leave without me. Yeah, I get it. If I'm not there don't wait. Go. If I make it out, we'll find you."

Elliot clasped his hand and pulled him in for a hug. He patted him on the back. "If this is the last time I see you…" he trailed off.

Damon gave a strained smile back. "Likewise."

With that said, Damon took off running at a crouch. Within minutes he disappeared into the shadows of the early morning. Elliot remained there for a minute or two longer before heading back inside. He was torn. On one hand he wanted to help but Gary needed him more. When he returned to the room, Gary was starting to stir.

"Uh," he groaned.

"How you feeling?"

"Like a truck rolled over me." He went to get up off

the couch and cried out in pain.

"You need pain medication. I'm taking you home. We're leaving in the next ten minutes."

Gary looked around the room. "Where's Damon?"

"Gone."

"He just upped and left?"

"No, I spoke to him before he took off."

Gary shook his head and scoffed. "He's going to get himself killed over a girl he doesn't even know. Idiot."

"Love is blind," Elliot replied, helping him to a seated position.

"That it is."

He helped Gary to his feet. "Let me take a look."

He lifted up Gary's top and his back was black and blue. He'd hit the ground with some force. There was no telling how many ribs he'd broken but his skin was showing some serious bruising. It had turned a gnarly shade of purple.

"We got anything to drink?"

"Yeah, Damon found some old juice boxes in the

basement. Not the best but they'll suffice." He went into the kitchen and grabbed up a couple and returned.

"When we get back to Lake Placid, we need to leave. You know that, don't you?" Gary said.

"Yeah. I already told him we won't be waiting. I said we would leave at six."

"We might have to leave sooner than that. There's no telling if Ella will tell them where we live."

Elliot nodded. He'd hoped to stay at least twenty-four hours to give Damon a chance to return but it wasn't exactly practical. Gary stuck a straw into the juice box and drained it dry. There was no food in the house and they hadn't eaten in twenty-four hours. His stomach grumbled and made odd noises. They'd grown accustomed to going long periods without food. At first it was difficult but the body soon adjusted. However that didn't make it any easier.

Once Gary was mentally ready for the long journey — a trip that would take over three hours by foot — they exited the home.

* * *

Dallas was feeling pretty damn good about the outcome. Two of those assholes were dead, they didn't manage to get the horses and he now had that bitch back right where he wanted her. This time she would remain in his sights. He'd had two of his men watch over her throughout the night while he slept nearby, and he'd posted six around the Rusty Nail and had the rest work the blockades and scour the surrounding streets within a three-mile radius. Of course he had them operate in rotating shifts to ensure they were well rested. The last thing he wanted was to die because they were exhausted.

He'd been awake staring at her from across the room for the past ten minutes. Dallas had slept on a soft leather couch. He pulled back a colorful blanket and swung his legs out and stretched.

"Good morning, sunshine!" Dallas said to her as he ambled over to the bar to make himself an early morning Bloody Mary. He pulled out MREs from a box and tossed several over to the guys guarding her. "Harris, go wake the others and have them take over your shifts. Get some food in you and some rest."

"Will do, boss."

He took off and Dallas motioned for the other guy to step outside so he could have some one-on-one time. He'd been eager to talk. He wanted her to understand why he was going to make her suffer. There was no fun in inflicting pain if the victim didn't know why. As the door closed behind his guy, he hopped up on the bar and began tucking into a chicken with egg noodles MRE. He scooped it into his mouth while eying her.

"You're probably hungry, right?" She didn't respond. "The quiet treatment. I get it." He sniffed. "I would offer you some but it would be a waste. You see, I want you to suffer but I want you to understand why you're going to suffer. Do you know?"

She glared at him. Dallas could see the hatred in her eyes.

"Well, if you're not going to talk I'll fill you in. Two months ago," he smacked his lips as he ate and talked at the same time, "you killed my brother." He paused. "You probably didn't know, hell, you probably don't even remember, right? I mean, why would you? He was just another threat." He wagged his plastic fork at her. "Though, I've got to say. I have to take my hat off to you. How you managed to elude us for two months is pretty damn impressive. There were others like you out there. Folks who thought they would be heroes. People who wouldn't listen to reason and join us so we had to kill them but you... um, you were like the fucking Energizer Bunny — you just kept on going, didn't you?" He stopped eating and stuck his tongue between his teeth to pick away some chicken that had got stuck. He sniffed and reached for his drink and took a sip. "So let me remind you. West side. Blond-haired kid. Blue eyes. He was wearing a black leather jacket with the emblem of a dragon. Ring any bells?"

Still no response.

"Anyway, you didn't just shoot him, did you? No, there was something about that killing that was personal.

You shot him in the kneecaps, and then used a knife. I counted roughly forty-one stab wounds. Overkill. So tell me, what drives a woman like you to inflict that kind of pain on someone you don't know?"

She spat in his direction.

"Geesh, you really have no off switch to that hate, do you? Let me guess, we killed your brother? Sister?" He tried to gauge her reaction as he spoke. "I know, your mother? Father, maybe?" She tensed up and he knew that was it. "Ah, revenge for us killing your parents." He chuckled. "You see I kind of find that funny really. You know why?"

She still didn't respond.

"You strike me as the kind of woman that left home early. Maybe seventeen? Am I right? You wanted to venture out and put your mark on the world and daddy dearest didn't like it. Am I getting close?"

She shuffled around, giving him a sense that she was uncomfortable.

"So why would you care if they were dead or alive?"

"I could ask you the same thing about your brother," she shot back.

He shook his fork at her. "A smart-ass. I like that." He took another drink. "I understand the whole eye for an eye, tooth for a tooth bullshit. It feels good, right? Doesn't it? Did you feel good after killing my brother?"

"Good? I felt amazing."

Dallas gripped his fork tight. He had a good mind to go over there and jab it in her eye and pluck it out of its socket and make her eat it. Instead, he dropped down from the bar and walked over and crouched near her. "Amazing? Um. Good choice of words. I was actually wondering what it was going to feel like when I'm done with you." He paused. "Amazing. That might encompass the feeling. I'm not sure. I guess I should get started."

With that said he dropped the fork into the bag and reached around for his serrated blade. He removed it slowly. He wanted her to see it. He wanted her to know what was coming next. There was no fun in going fast. The body couldn't fully appreciate the depth of what it was about to feel if it was rushed. No, he wanted to see the fear in her eyes. Dallas grabbed a hold of her foot, and cut away the laces until the boot came off in his hand. He tossed it to one side as he then removed her sock. "That's a good-looking foot. Pity." He ran the tip of the blade over her skin and stared into her eyes as he pressed harder, slicing at the skin then pulling the knife away.

"Fuck you!" she said, in a final act of defiance.

"Back atcha!" he said before driving the knife down into her foot slowly. He held her ankle tight so she couldn't pull away. Her cries were ear-piercing, and they only got worse when he extracted it and the serrated edge tore at her skin. Once he pulled it out, he waved the knife in front of her face. "Did your mother ever let you lick the icing off the mixing stick? Care for a taste?" He laughed and slid the knife back into his sheath, rose and walked back to the bar to get his drink.

"Just kill me and get it over with," she said.

"Oh I'm not going to rush this, darlin'. You don't rush these kinds of things. No, it's like making a good cup of coffee. You got to give it time to brew. No, this is going to be an interesting day." He chuckled. "Actually it's amazing how many ideas come to you in the middle of the night. But I don't want to hog all the ideas. So if you have any, I'm all ears. Me? I would love to share with you what I've got in store but where would the fun be in that? It's the anticipation of Christmas that gets us excited, right?"

He took his place at the bar and finished eating breakfast while she wailed in pain behind him. Every now and again he would glance at her in the bar's mirror and smile. *Oh, this was going to be good.*

* * *

Samuel Hayes stood outside with the others that morning around 6 a.m. as they did roll call. Shelby said it was to ensure that no one else had died in another attack, but that wasn't it. He just wanted to make sure no one had escaped.

He looked on in horror at his brother's beaten body hanging by his wrists from the pole at the center of the yard. A tear rolled down his cheek. He knew that he was responsible.

He thought he'd end up in the sweatbox, not beaten within an inch of his life.

Shelby had a bandage wrapped around his head.

"Well it looks like everyone is here," Shelby said through his megaphone. "Now before you go, I thought it would be best to explain why this man here is being punished. As you know my aim is to provide freedom and to ensure those rights aren't infringed upon by the government or any other group that's out there. And to ensure your safety I have had to take matters into my own hands since the death of five of my men. This man you see before you, murdered them. Let me put that in perspective — the same people that were protecting you, he murdered them. Now I know you're probably wondering, why should you care? It's simple. We are the ones protecting you. And an attack on my men is an attack on you. There is no telling if he would have killed one of you and I certainly wasn't going to wait until he did. That's why he's hanging there. And so if there is anyone else thinking of turning on us, let this be an example. Punishment will be swift and severe."

Shelby fixed his gaze on Samuel. Samuel wiped the tears from his face but it was too late. He'd seen them.

"Today we will continue working on the wall to patch it up. I will also be having a group of you go out with ten of my men to hunt for food."

"Hunt. But we have more than enough?" someone called out.

"Yes. Yes we do. However, those supplies dwindle every day, and we have even more mouths to feed. As you will come to learn, our group is very proactive. We don't wait until the last minute before taking action, and neither should you." His words couldn't have been clearer. Samuel continued to stare at Ryan. He wasn't looking at him. His head was drooping. Every so often it looked like he attempted to raise it but couldn't. After everyone was dismissed, Samuel approached Shelby.

"Samuel. How can I help?"

"You said you would treat him fairly."

"And I did."

"By beating him?"

Shelby waved away his men. "Walk with me, Samuel."

Samuel fell in step.

"I don't have to remind you that we are living in dangerous times. In order to survive, hard decisions must be made. I'm not looking to win the admiration of anyone, neither will my actions be understood but rest assured, there is purpose behind them."

"How long is he going to hang there?"

"That's not your concern."

"He's still my brother."

"And he's a killer. Let's not forget that. What would you have me do? Pamper him, lock him in a cell? What kind of message does that send to anyone else who might be considering walking in his shoes?"

"I thought you were going to place him in the sweatbox, like Timothy."

"The punishment matches the crime. Do we place

those who have murdered in a halfway house or in a maximum security prison?"

"Then how long are you going to keep him there?"

"For as long as I deem it necessary."

"Which is?"

He stopped walking. "Do you know what else he did?"

Samuel looked at the bloody bandage.

"Let me show you."

Shelby reached up and began to unravel the bandage. Once the final piece came off, it revealed a messed-up piece of skin hanging from his face. It was red and bloodied and completely raw.

"That's right. He did that. I could have shot your brother. The fact that he is still alive is because I am fair. So don't question me about what I should or shouldn't do. Just fall in line and ask what you can do. Do I make myself clear?"

Samuel nodded. With that said, Shelby walked away leaving him to gaze upon his brother. He considered approaching him but the guilt was eating him up.

Chapter 19

Long before the sun rose, Jesse had been riding the streets of Lake Placid searching for that white Chevy truck that had been stolen from the police department a few months ago. He figured that whoever had taken it only had a few options for hiding it. Either it was inside a garage or concealed by a vehicle tarp. Using a mountain bike and the cover of darkness he'd been riding up and down streets in the hope of locating it. They could have used bikes to reach Saranac Lake that morning but that truck would have been real handy. He hadn't told anyone when he left in the dead of night. Now, with the sun coming up, he'd all but given up, until he spotted it on the south side of town in an area where few people might have looked. He almost shot by it but caught it in his peripheral vision. After slamming on the brakes, he wheeled around and ditched his bike in a thicket of trees before bringing around his AR-15. As nervous as he was, there was a lot riding on this. As the sun broke over the trees he glanced down at his watch. It was close to six-thirty. They knew two men were using it as they'd encountered them on several occasions, usually after they had set fire to homes and stolen property.

Quickly, Jesse moved at a crouch through the trees surrounding the two-story white clapboard home. It had a white wraparound porch, black shingles and an American flag blowing in the breeze outside. His eyes scanned the windows looking for movement. He was pretty sure they wouldn't leave keys in the vehicle and Damon had never shown him how to hotwire a car. In between the trees he could see the vehicle. His heart hammered in his chest. The exhilaration of finding it, and the anticipation of a confrontation kept him on his toes.

Shadows stretched across the lawn under the morning light. The chirping of birds in the trees, and the crunch of grass and gravel beneath his feet was all that could be heard. Jesse got as close as he could to the vehicle before darting out of the tree line and slamming his back into the truck. Breathing fast, he snuck a peek around the corner of the truck to check if he'd been spotted. So far so good. He readjusted his grip on the rifle and peered into the truck. He tried the door and it opened but sure enough there were no keys in the ignition. *No surprise there.* Still, he checked the center console and the glove compartment, as well as the sun visors before slipping out and heading towards the house. That morning he was wearing a ballistic vest and a SWAT helmet that he'd acquired from the department. His clothes were all black. On his back he had the words POLICE in white. It wasn't his first choice of clothing but it was comfortable and light and easy to move in. He'd brought with him a hunting knife, a Glock 17 with two magazines, two smoke grenades and an AR-15 with three magazines. He expected to run into trouble and so was fully prepared.

He made his way up onto the back porch. He peered through one of the windows into a living room. It was rustic but elegant in appearance with cathedral-style ceilings, wood paneling and a large roaring fireplace at the far end. He tried the back door but it was locked. Holding his rifle low he moved forward, checking windows as he went. All of them were sealed tight. Whoever was inside wasn't taking any chances. The front, rear and back doors were locked. He backed up from the house and figured he'd give the single red door on the north side of the home a try. It was located on the second floor. To reach it, he swung his rifle around his back and climbed up the porch and hauled himself over the lip of the balcony. As soon as he made it to the top, he waited another minute to be sure that no one had heard him before approaching and turning the knob. Again nothing. He was close to smashing a window when he gave the second-floor window a try.

At last — it shifted!

He slid the window up and ducked inside, dropping slowly to the floor and peering around the room. He saw a double bed that hadn't been slept in, a high-end floor rug, two side tables and a few pieces of Adirondack-style furniture. Other than that, it was empty. Although he moved slowly the hardwood floor still creaked. Every time it did, he held his breath, keeping the gun trained on the door in anticipation.

His pulse raced, and beads of sweat formed on his brow.

He stayed calm, moving slowly until he worked his way out to the hallway that overlooked the living room below. That's when he saw them — five men, asleep.

Shit.

They were positioned around the corner from the ground floor window. That's why he hadn't seen them. Had he known, there was no chance in hell he would have risked it. He would have waited until they left in the truck and followed them but now he was in the lion's den.

Right then he heard the creak of a floorboard and an adjacent door to a bedroom across the hallway opened. A man came out yawning, the belt on his jeans undone, and pawing at his eyes. He took one look at Jesse, and the shit hit the fan.

Jesse didn't hesitate pulling the trigger.

He fired off one round. It struck the guy in the chest sending him stumbling back. Jesse released his rifle, grabbed a smoke grenade, gave it a pull and tossed it over the banister down into the living room. The five men, startled by the gun going off, were trying to get a bead on him when the red smoke filled the air, causing even more confusion. Jesse used it to his advantage and unleashed a torrent of rounds. Even though his aim had improved over the last six months, most weren't accurate but three dropped, a fourth was injured and trying to return fire while the fifth bolted out the back door.

All around him wood spat and splinters flew as rounds tore up the paneling.

Smoke made it hard to see the fourth guy but it also blocked his view of Jesse.

An engine roared to life, and Jesse darted back into the room and out of the window. The white truck reversed and spun around preparing to exit the driveway. Although he didn't want to risk destroying the truck, he had to stop the driver before he vanished. Jesse brought up the rifle just as the guy slammed his foot on the accelerator and the truck surged forward.

Pop. Pop. Pop. The rounds lanced the windshield, the driver swerved and slammed into a tree. Jesse was about to climb down when a bullet struck him in the back. He crashed to the floor of the balcony, turning in time to see the man he'd shot climbing out of the window. His rifle had fallen out of his hands and he was now lying on his side. As the guy fired again, the round missed and a chunk of wood hit Jesse in the face. Reaching for his Glock strapped to his thigh, he returned fire as another round from his attacker skimmed his shoulder. Jesse squeezed off round after round, four shots in rapid succession, each one hitting its mark, two in the chest, and two in the abdomen. Unfortunately for his attacker, he wasn't wearing a vest like Jesse.

His legs buckled and Jesse heard him take his last few breaths.

Gasping on his back, Jesse touched his shoulder. The

round hadn't gone through but had nicked it. The ballistic vest stopped the one that had hit him in the back. He groaned. Even though he was protected by the vest, being struck by a bullet still hurt. He staggered to his feet and looked over the balcony. The driver of the truck hadn't got out, and the engine was idling.

Jesse climbed down, and cautiously approached the vehicle.

There was no need to worry. One look and it was clear the guy was dead.

One of the rounds had struck him in the throat. He was slumped over the wheel.

Jesse dragged him out and dumped his body to the side of the road and then walked down to collect his bike. He dropped it in the back, shut off the engine and then returned to the house to collect weapons, ammo and whatever else might be of use. As he gazed around at the dead bodies and chugged down a can of Budweiser, he felt his confidence rise. Gathering what he could from the house, he peeled out of the driveway heading for home with a sense of accomplishment.

* * *

Roughly one hour later on the outskirts of Saranac Lake, Jesse spotted the two of them. Elliot was holding up Gary and both of them looked exhausted. At first they must have thought they were in trouble as they hurried into the woodland to the north of Highway 86. As they got closer, Jesse veered off and Maggie called out to them.

Minutes later they sank into the warmth of the rear seats while Clive Robins and two other men got in the back.

"Where's Damon?" Jesse asked.

"Just head back," Elliot said in an exhausted manner.

"Is he dead?"

"No."

"Then where is he?"

"Jesse, just listen to me. Gary needs medical attention. Go. I'll explain on the way."

He swerved around, glancing down the road towards a sign for Saranac Lake before heading back to Lake Placid.

On the way Elliot brought him up to speed on what had happened. Sean and Zach were dead, Ella was captured and Damon was going it alone.

"You left him there?"

"I had no choice. It was that or leave Gary."

Jesse slammed his fist against the wheel.

"I'll drop you off and then Clive and the rest of us will go back."

"No. It's too dangerous. There are too many of them."

"Then how the hell is he going to survive?"

"He made the call, Jesse. He knows the risk."

"And that's it? We're just going to leave him?"

"You have no idea who or what we were up against. I don't like it any more than you but my concern is for Gary, then getting out of Lake Placid."

"And leave him behind?"

"We have no choice."

"You said we always have a choice."

Elliot looked at him. Gary groaned in agony. The pain seemed to have intensified.

"I'm not having this discussion now."

"Of course not," Jesse said clenching his jaw. "Well you might be okay with leaving him behind but I'm not."

"He can take care of himself."

"Bullshit!"

Elliot didn't respond any further. He glanced out the window looking off into the distance. When they returned, Rayna was there to meet them.

Neither Maggie nor Jesse told Elliot what had happened to Jill or Rayna. Rayna had told Maggie not to say anything about the rape, and to let her tell Gary about Jill. What she didn't expect was to see him in the state he was when they pulled into the driveway. Elliot was the first out.

"Rayna. Give me a hand," Elliot said.

Gary's moaning got worse as they carried him down into the bunker so Elliot could treat his wounds. There was very little that could be done for broken ribs. Although it was painful, it was a common injury but without being able to take an X-ray they had to hope that none of the blood vessels or internal organs had been damaged. Best case scenario was he was looking at a good two months of recovery time, and chewing a shitload of pain medication.

"Where's Jill?" Gary asked.

"Rest up," Rayna said covering him with a blanket.

She tapped Elliot on the arm and he told Gary that he'd be back to check on him. Outside, Jesse and Maggie watched from a distance as Rayna talked with Elliot. They could only guess what she was telling him.

Chapter 20

Ella's screams could be heard long before Damon had the Rusty Nail in his sights. He tightened his grip on the rifle and tried to stop his imagination from running wild. *What was he doing?* Damon crouched behind a tree. He snuck a peek knowing that going in was suicide. He'd contemplated throughout the night different ways of tackling the problem. He'd considered turning himself in and pledging allegiance to his group, in the hopes that he'd take him onboard as one of his men, but that idea fell by the wayside. They'd killed too many of his group. He wouldn't buy it. Dallas would probably execute him or assume it was just a setup. And even if he didn't, the chances of Damon getting near Ella would be slim to none. That didn't leave many options. He could grab one of his men and use him as leverage to do an exchange but chances were Dallas would rather see his own men die than hand Ella over. They were nothing but a means to an end. Magnus had been proof of that.

Then of course there was the hope that Elliot would have a change of heart and return but even if he did, it could be hours before he returned. Another scream cut through him like a cold wind. He couldn't wait. She'd be dead by then.

His only option was to kill as many of Dallas's men as possible before they realized they were being taken out. He wished it were night so he could use the cover of darkness. It would have been a hell of a lot easier but he had to go with the cards he'd been dealt.

* * *

Dallas loved every minute of it. He had Ella strung up by her wrists. The rope was slung over a thick wooden ceiling beam and tied off behind the bar. He had taken a hunting knife and torn down the back of her shirt exposing her bare skin so he could whip her with cable taken from the lighting equipment in the bar.

He stepped back to admire his work. Her back was red and raw with stripes that cut into the skin. He was sweating from whipping her for five minutes straight. Each time she passed out from the pain he would splash wine on her face.

Her head hung low and she groaned.

"It's amazing, isn't it? You know, what the body can withstand," he said.

Dallas took a swig of his beer.

"I imagine by now you are wondering where your friends are?" He lit a cigarette, blew smoke out his nostrils then circled her. He smiled, satisfied that she was receiving a punishment that was worthy of her crime. "I know I would be." He nodded and took another drag before sniffing hard. "Well I hate to piss on your fire but I don't think they're coming. In fact I got word from one of the blockades on the east side that two of them were seen limping away, heading for Lake Placid, I believe. Does that sound right?" He got close to her and blew smoke in her face, then took a swig of his beer.

"I remember," she mumbled. It was so quiet he barely heard her.

"What?"

"I said I remember."

"Remember what?"

"Killing your brother."

He gritted his teeth. "Go on."

"Yeah. It's all coming back to me." She raised her head, her face swollen from multiple beatings. "Begged for his life." She snorted. "He was a real pussy. I'm guessing the apple doesn't fall far from the tree."

Dallas felt a swell of rage. He tossed the beer across the room and grabbed her by the throat. "I was going to kill you by the end of today. Not now. I'm going to keep you alive as long as I can. I'm going to draw this out until you are begging me to kill you. And when you do, I'll keep going for a few more days. Then I'm going to gut you like a pig."

He released his grip and walked back over to the bar and grasped the cable, took one more drag on his cigarette and then returned to whipping her. Her screams tore through the bar and once again he felt better.

* * *

From the top of the bowling alley roof, Damon observed the bar through the binoculars belonging to one of Dallas's now deceased men. He knew Dallas would be on high alert and expecting them to attack, which was why he aimed to draw them away. He scanned the perimeter, then directed the binoculars at the building called Little City Hair Cutters. Any moment now they would see the flames.

"Come on, move!" he muttered raking the binoculars. Thick black smoke started to rise to the south of them. He was located to east. The fire was there simply to create a diversion. He didn't expect it would draw away all of them and that wasn't his intention. All he wanted to see was how many there were, where they were positioned and how they would react.

Now he knew there was a sniper in the home across from the bar. He was the next one on his list. It would also give him a way to take out those standing outside. The way he saw it, as long as they didn't see him, and he created enough confusion, he could increase the odds of being able to get close without being spotted.

Smoke moved like a ghostly apparition down the streets.

Sure enough, there they were, like rats crawling out of the woodwork. He watched as they emerged from their spots to see what was happening. One. Two. C'mon, there had to be more. Three. Four. If there were more, he couldn't see them. The homes were blocking his view. He watched as two of them took off to see what was happening.

Climbing down from Romano's Saranac Lanes building, he sprinted through the back alleys toward H&R Block on the north side. Again he went through the process of breaking in and starting a fire. It was all about distractions, confusion and drawing them away so he could get close to the home across the street. Damon had come up with a plan that worked in phases. This was phase one, distraction. Phase two was killing the sniper. He didn't have a phase three because he didn't know if he'd be alive by that point. However, so far things were going well.

Smoke billowed high into a gunmetal sky.

He could hear voices and see men running to check out what was happening.

Damon shifted behind the home of the sniper. He entered through an unlocked door at the back and moved quietly through the house, climbing the steps. With his Glock in one hand and a hunting knife in the other he stayed composed and calm even though his pulse was racing. As he was ascending the steps, he kept his feet to the outside. In an old home, the outer rim of the steps was usually the strongest and less likely to squeak. As he made it to the top, he could hear the guy talking on the radio.

"What's going on down there?"

A crackle and a voice replied, "We're looking into it."

"You have orders not to move."

"Ah fuck Dallas, if these assholes are back with more people, I'm not dying for him."

Damon stifled a laugh. It didn't matter who they were, people were people at the end of the day. Loyalty only went so far and in a collapsed society where you could be dead before the end of the day, no one was going to lose their head for one guy. It didn't matter what he offered.

"Keep me updated," the sniper said. As Damon rounded the corner he could see him. He had a beard and was wearing a thin jacket, camo pants and a ballistic vest. He'd positioned himself just in from the window. The rifle wasn't sticking out, and that's why they hadn't spotted him. Damon had done well reaching the second level without alerting him. That all ended when one of the hardwood floorboards creaked.

"Jason?" the man called out.

Damon knew he had less than a few seconds to react. If he got on that radio the place would be swarming with men. Damon charged in with his Glock raised just as the man reached for the radio.

"Put it down!"

He would have shot him but he was trying to avoid

drawing attention.

The guy raised his hands slowly. "Look, man, I don't want to die."

"Then put the fucking radio down."

He nodded and set it down.

"Slide it over here, and your weapon."

The guy complied, his eyes never breaking from Damon's.

"And your handgun." He reached for it. "Slowly!" Damon said. He tossed it and Damon told him to put his hands behind his back and remain laying on the bed. The bed had been pushed up close to the window and he'd been laying on it so he could relax and keep an eye on anyone approaching the bar.

"Look, I was just following orders."

Damon moved in quickly and placed a knee on his back. He pushed the Glock to the back of his head. "How many are there?"

"Six."

"And the others?"

"Looking for you all."

"How many?"

He shrugged. Damon slapped him with the gun's barrel. "How many?" he asked again in a firmer tone.

"Twenty, maybe thirty... I guess."

"Well which is it?"

"Roughly around twenty. I don't exactly keep track of them all. Look, man, I don't want to die."

Damon placed his gun into his holster and tightened his grip on the knife.

"No one does."

With that said he reached around and slit his throat and held him there until he bled out. He knew if the shoe were on the other foot he would have done the same. Once the guy was dead, he scooped up the radio, his additional weapons and ammo, and then rolled him off the bed. He got close to the window and snuck a peek. There were only three outside. He hurried over to the sniper's rifle and brought it up, he positioned himself so that the rifle's barrel was resting on the window frame.

He squinted, and brought his other eye up to the scope and got one of the men in the crosshair. He had to be quick and then get out before the others returned. Every round had to count.

He took a deep breath and exhaled as he squeezed the trigger.

The first one dropped, the second followed seconds after and the third he caught as he tried to make a break for it. Damon slung the rifle over his shoulder and bolted out, leaving behind the man in a puddle of blood.

With the coast clear he changed his plans.

The goal wasn't to kill them all, only those that could prevent him from getting inside. Damon darted out of the home and crossed the street. He burst into the bar with the Glock raised.

* * *

Minutes before the gunfire, Ella coughed and spluttered from having more wine splashed in her face. Another shot of pain coursed through her body. She'd tried to get her hands loose, but it was useless. He'd made damn sure she wasn't going anywhere.

As the sound of gunfire erupted, she raised her swollen face and tried to make out what was happening. It was hard to see anything through blurred vision.

Was it them? Damon?

Whoever it was, it had caught the attention of Dallas. He was standing by the window looking out when blood splattered against the pane of glass. Two more shots echoed, and Dallas stumbled back, a look of fear on his face. He didn't say anything to her but hurried over to the bar and pulled out a sawed-off shotgun from behind it.

Not wasting any time he crossed the room and placed it against her head. She thought he was going to pull the trigger. If he had she wouldn't have cared. She was done with the pain and suffering. All she wanted to do was join her parents.

That's when the door burst open and she caught sight of him.

Damon!

"That's far enough!" Dallas yelled. Damon closed the

door behind him and locked it. His eyes bounced from Dallas to her. "I'll kill her."

"No you won't," Damon said. "Otherwise you would have done it by now."

He stepped forward and was warned again.

"You get any closer and I pull the trigger."

"You can't shoot both of us. If she dies, so do you," he replied. "I would think long and hard about that if I was you."

From outside, men could be heard yelling. Someone approached the door and rattled the knob.

"Dallas?" a deep booming voice called out.

Instead of replying Dallas continued, "You kill me, you're dead too."

"Maybe."

"Then how do you expect to get out of here?"

"Who said anything about getting out of here?"

Dallas looked at him, narrowed his eyes then glanced at Ella. He must have thought Damon was out of his mind. Perhaps he was.

They eyed each other with contempt.

"You're alone, aren't you?" Dallas said.

"Well I'm sure your men will find out in," he glanced at his watch, "about four minutes."

"You're bluffing," Dallas said, shifting nearer to her.

"Am I?" Damon replied.

There was a long pause; Dallas glanced up at the clock. He was waiting to see what would happen as the seconds ticked over. Through slitted eyes, Ella looked at Damon. She couldn't believe he'd come back for her. If it was just him, he was insane.

"Let her go."

"It's not happening."

There was more silence. Minutes passed. Outside more of his group arrived. He could hear them beating against the door.

"It doesn't have to end here."

"Of course it does." Dallas smiled, then looked at the clock. "Your four minutes are up," he said with a hint of glee.

"Ah, maybe it was ten."

"And maybe you are full of shit!"

"It doesn't change the fact that you aren't walking out of this bar alive."

"You've got it all backwards," Dallas said beginning to laugh. "You think I want to live, don't you?"

"Do you?"

It was a like card game, a back and forth between them to see which one would break or give away his hand. Another shot of excruciating pain went through her. Several salty tears rolled into her mouth. She never thought her life would end here.

"She killed my brother."

"We've all killed someone's brother," Damon replied.

There was a pause as if both of them were contemplating. Ella knew this wasn't going anywhere fast and knowing Dallas wasn't going to drop that gun, she was fully prepared for what came next. Using what little energy she could summon, she lifted her knees and swung her body against Dallas. Her goal wasn't to knock him over but to create a momentary distraction, enough that…

A round exploded, she only heard one shot.

Chapter 21

By late morning, Frank Shelby was staring in a mirror at his mutilated ear. It was beginning to look infected. He soaked a cloth in hydrogen peroxide and dabbed it gently against the mangled, bloody tissue. Frank winced as it stung.

There was a knock at the door.

"Hold on a minute."

He turned and retrieved the new bandage and wrapped it around his head. He didn't want anyone gawking at it. Frank gritted his teeth. Hatred for Ryan Hayes welled up inside. He was going to have to grow his hair long now to hide it.

Another knock.

"I said one minute."

Once he was done, he opened the door to find Samuel.

"Yes?"

"I was hoping to have a moment of your time."

"Come on in."

He closed the door, went around his desk and collected a glass and a bottle of bourbon. "Drink?"

"No, but thank you."

Frank poured himself three fingers. "What can I do for you?"

Samuel took a seat. "You told me to tell you if I heard of anyone trying to go against you. Well, I have but you're not going to like it."

"I'll determine that. Who is it?"

Without missing a beat Samuel said, "Your brother."

Frank spat his drink out, then wiped his mouth with the back of his sleeve.

He placed the glass down and scowled. "You're lying."

"No I'm not, I heard him this morning talking with several of your men. They believe you're going to create an uprising by punishing people. They are planning to relieve you of your rank."

Frank shook his head, and he scowled.

"Bullshit."

"Call for him. Ask him yourself," Samuel said with an air of confidence.

He was either lying, which wouldn't end well, or he was telling the truth. Frank had knocked heads with his brother John on a number of occasions over the years. It had always been the same. John had bought into the idea of standing against the government and anyone who opposed Frank, but when it came down to it, he was always the first to try and get the men to consider other options. Even before they raided the compound, he'd been trying to talk Frank out of it. He'd even managed to get thirteen of his forty-six men to vote against it. It wasn't enough, but it was proof that perhaps there was some truth to what Samuel was saying. He couldn't believe his own brother would go against him. Didn't he understand what he was building here?

Samuel stared straight ahead, unfazed by having told him.

Frank raised a finger. "If you are lying…"

"Yeah, I already know. But don't expect him to just

come out with it."

"Then how can I know?"

"He's your brother. I knew when mine was lying," Samuel replied.

He had a point.

Frank approached the door and told one of his men posted outside to go get John.

He returned and closed the door behind him.

"If you're lying…"

"Why would I lie? What do I have to gain? You're in control."

Frank nodded. "Damn right I am."

He took another swig of his drink and studied him, trying to find a crack in his facade. Frank wasn't sure how to respond to his allegations. The only reason he found it hard to believe was because even though John had gone against him a few times when the group had to make hard decisions, he was his brother. His own flesh and blood wouldn't do that. A few minutes passed before John stepped inside.

"You wanted to see me?"

Frank beckoned him in. "Close the door."

He glanced at Samuel before turning his attention back to Frank.

"You got something to tell me?" Frank asked casually. He didn't want to give him a sense that he was against him. A look of confusion spread across John's face.

He shrugged. "No, why?"

"You sure?"

"Positive," he glanced away and looked at Samuel again as if trying to connect the dots. "What's going on here, Frank?"

"So?" Frank asked Samuel.

"I'm telling the truth."

John's brow furrowed. "What the fuck is going on, Frank?"

"Samuel here informs me that you and some of the men are considering relieving me of my rank. Essentially, taking over."

John's brow pinched, then he lunged at Samuel, a fist

connecting with his face knocking him into the wall. "Why you bastard! I'm gonna…"

Before he could get any more jabs in, Frank pulled him back. John shrugged him off.

"So there's truth to it then?" Frank asked.

"No! He's lying."

"No I'm not," Samuel said, spitting blood.

John lunged at him again but was quickly restrained and forced up against a wall.

He threw up his hands. "I swear, Frank. I would never do that. He's lying."

Samuel wiped at his bloody lip. "Why would I lie to you when I didn't lie about my own brother? I could have said nothing. Done nothing. He's suffered because of my actions. My loyalty. I went against my own flesh and blood for you, Frank."

Again he made a strong argument. What did he have to gain by lying? He would have only put himself at risk. He sighed. Frank didn't know who to believe. If his brother hadn't already fought him at every turn on decisions, he would have believed him but he had bitched and complained about every single action he wanted to take.

"I swear, Frank. Ask the men. They'll back me up."

"I bet they will."

John scowled. "I don't understand." He was at a loss for words. "You're taking his word over mine? Your own brother?"

"Wasn't it Cain who killed Abel?" Frank shot back.

They'd grown up in a religious family. Living in the Bible belt of the nation it was hard to avoid it.

"You're out of your mind. If you let him get in your head, then we are done here."

"Are we?"

Frank didn't like his tone. He went to the door and opened it, asked two of his men to escort John out. They entered and took a hold of him and dragged him kicking and yelling. "What the hell, Frank?"

"Maybe you need some time to remember. Put him in the sweatbox."

"Frank!" His voice echoed as he was dragged away.

Once the door was closed, Frank took a seat behind his desk and drained what was left of his drink. He ran a tired hand over his face. He wasn't getting much sleep and the last thing he needed to deal with was a bad apple among his own group.

"I said you weren't going to like it. What are you going to do with him?" Samuel asked.

"I haven't decided. I need to talk with my men."

"If he isn't going to tell you, do you think they are?"

Again, another good point. Frank scratched at his stubble.

"And what do you suppose I do?"

Samuel leaned back. "You're asking for my advice?"

"Not advice. What would you do?"

He sat there for a minute or two thinking about it.

"Keep them busy."

"What?"

"People with too much time on their hands, think too much. Keep them busy."

"Doing what?"

"Mend the wall, scavenge for more supplies and…" Samuel trailed off.

Frank replied, "And?"

Samuel shifted in his seat. "Train us to fight. At the end of the day, general, your enemies are mine."

He was cold and callous. But Frank liked that. It reminded him of himself. He wasn't sure what to make of Samuel. One thing for sure, Frank liked to be referred to as general. His acknowledgement of his rank showed respect, and his honesty had already thwarted two takeover attempts. Okay, the second was still to be determined but he had a sense that he was telling the truth. He'd already thrown his own brother under the bus in order to prove his loyalty. What else did he have to prove?

* * *

Outside, after leaving Shelby's office, Samuel felt a wave of confidence. It had worked. He'd bought it. Samuel nodded to a soldier on his way back from escorting Frank's brother away. After collecting a bottle of water, he made his way outside into the yard and over to his brother who hung limp from the post. No one stopped him because who in their right mind would try to release him when armed guards patrolled on the walls? A hard Texas sun bore down as Samuel got closer to his brother. There were few clouds in the blue sky that stretched over them. Samuel dragged over a log that was positioned by a nearby campfire. He turned it vertical and stood on it to reach his brother's lips.

"Here you go, Ryan," he said bringing the bottle up to his dry, cracked lips.

Ryan swallowed slowly at first but then took more.

"Slow down. It's okay."

As he was drinking from the bottle, Samuel got real close.

"It worked, brother. It worked." He removed the bottle from his lips and screwed the cap back on. He gripped his hand. "It won't be long and we'll take this compound back."

"And if they won't fight?" Ryan muttered.

"I'll find people that will. I promise."

Ryan nodded but said nothing as Samuel dropped down and dragged the log back to where it had been. As he walked away, his mind drifted back to the conversation he'd had with his brother, the night he was taken. *"Then join me. Work with me, brother, to take them down from the inside," Ryan had said.* Samuel had thought long and hard about those words after leaving his room. Two hours later he'd returned, and that's when they hatched the plan to earn Frank's trust in order to take him down from the inside. Turning over Ryan was just par for the course. It was a huge risk, and one that could have cost them their lives, but if it meant freedom, it was a price they were both willing to pay.

* * *

Damon held Ella's limp body in his arms after cutting her down. He didn't get to say goodbye. Although no tears were shed in that moment, he couldn't help but feel the loss. He ran a hand over her blood-splattered cheek and closed her eyelids. Behind him angry fists beat on the door calling for Dallas. They wouldn't get an answer. A few feet away, Dallas lay motionless, peppered with slugs.

It occurred so fast.

Ella moved.

Dallas pulled the trigger.

And Damon reacted by unloading four rounds into his frame. Dallas twisted and collapsed, dying instantly.

"Dallas!" a gruff voice bellowed outside.

Several rounds were fired at the door. Wood spat in every direction. Damon knew within a matter of minutes they'd come bursting in and it would be over. He was ready to die if need be. He'd been ready to die as far back as his time in Rikers. Damon wasn't afraid of death. It was coming whether he liked it or not.

Damon turned and fired a few rounds at the door to hold back the tide for a few more minutes. He looked down at Ella one last time before rising to his feet. He exhaled hard and ambled over to the bar and took a bottle of bourbon, twisted the top and chugged it down before wiping his lips. He gazed around looking for exit points. Besides the two doors at the front, there was one side door. There were no windows except at the front. He figured they were guarding all three spots, just waiting for him to emerge.

"Well I guess this is it."

He took a deep breath and his eyes washed over the bottles of whiskey, rum and bourbon. Behind him he could hear a generator churning over. That's when an idea came to him. There was a fifty-fifty chance of him surviving but at least if he was going out, he planned on taking a few with him. Damon fired the remainder of his Glock's magazine at the door and windows to buy him some time. Glass shattered as they returned fire. He slid over the bar, grabbed a few of the empty bottles from a recyclable trashcan and hurried toward the rear to locate the generator. He could have used one hundred percent rum but any lower than that and there was a chance it wouldn't work. Once he located the rumbling generator, he switched it off and removed the cap which held the diesel and then kicked it over. It hit the ground hard and diesel fluid splashed out. He took the bottles and began filling as many as he could from the liquid now draining out. He created seven Molotov cocktails. He tore off his shirt and used it to create some rags that he tucked it into each bottle.

Damon carried them and set them on the bar, then fired a few more rounds with his AR-15 at the walls, windows and doors. He ducked as drywall spat all over the place and rounds tore up the décor. He had only one goal, and that was to make it hard for them to see him exit. After lighting the rags on two, he grabbed the bottles and rushed towards the shattered windows and tossed them out in different directions. He raced back and did the same with two more though this time kicking one of the front doors open and lobbing them out.

Outside, fire smothered the ground and black smoke rose.

He grabbed two more and opened the side door and threw them out.

Gunfire erupted from every direction as they tried to get a bead on him. He snatched up the last cocktail, gave one last glance at Ella and then tossed it at the front of the bar. It exploded and tongues of flame licked up the wood, catching the wall and bar afire. He made a dash for the side exit, running out into a smoke-filled sky. He squeezed off rounds in rapid succession, striking one of them before climbing up a short wall that let him get on the bar's incline roof. Once on that he climbed onto the grassy slope behind it. Those who spotted him fired at him. A bullet struck him between the shoulder blades. He gasped but there was no time to stay put. Even though he was wearing a ballistic vest, pain shot through him. Damon kept moving, scrambling up the steep incline, his pulse hammering hard as he darted between the trees returning fire and tried to make his escape.

Behind him, he heard women and men yelling.

He had no idea how many were outside, or how many would follow, but he wouldn't risk taking a look over his shoulder. Damon turned on the jets, his knees pumping like pistons.

He scanned his field of vision and kept running, darting between trees, crossing roads and going around homes. Occasionally he took cover behind vehicles to see if anyone was coming but he never stayed in one spot long.

All that mattered now was getting home.

Chapter 22

A warm band of summer light filtered through pine trees as the sun rose over Lake Placid the next morning. Elliot placed the last duffel bag into the back of the white Chevy truck and looked toward Jesse who waited by the side of the road holding out hope for Damon's return. It was nearly six and as promised they were about to embark on a long journey for the compound in Texas. Elliot cast a glance at Gary who sat inside the truck, his head leaning against the passenger side window. Shock would have been the best way to describe his reaction to the news of Jill's death. No tears were shed, nor was he inconsolable, instead, he simply retreated inward. There was no way to know what was going through his mind, or how it would affect him. Everyone dealt with loss in different ways. However, when asked if he still wanted to go to the FEMA camp, he simply shook his head and replied, "Not now."

Kong trotted over with Lily and Evan, and took a piss beside the driveway, as if marking his territory just in case they ever returned. After, he hopped into the back of the truck bed and joined Clive and his wife, Wendy, Brianna, Tristan Summers and her child, Brian Hanson and Thomas Walsh. They were the only ones that would be joining them. Although initially some of the neighbors along the street had shown an interest in going, when it came down to it, they went back on that decision. As crazy as it might seem, there would always be those that couldn't envision life beyond their hometown. Their memories were there, family was there, and if they couldn't survive, then they would accept their fate.

Elliot didn't hold it against them. Besides, it would have been hard to feed them all.

They assumed the journey to East Texas would take anywhere from two to five days, depending on what problems they faced — so they'd packed enough provisions to see them through a round-trip just in case.

"Clive, did you remember the extra gasoline?"

"We're sitting on it," he said getting up with the others and pulling back a thick coat to reveal three large gas cans.

Elliot patted the side of the truck. "Good. Maggie, how about ammo and weapons?"

"I've checked it three times. Trust me. I know what I'm doing."

Rayna was the last to join them. She'd wanted to gather a few belongings, photos mainly, and the children's keepsakes. She adjusted the bag over her shoulder and gave a strained smile as she placed it in the back.

"How long's he been waiting by the road?" she asked looking at Jesse.

"Since four this morning."

"You think he made it?"

"I don't know," Elliot said. "If anyone could, Damon would."

She turned and looked at Gary. "Does he blame me?"

"I never told him how it went down, only that you were both jumped."

"What?"

He turned his head toward her. "You expect me to tell him that Jill wanted to leave, but you wanted to help some girl who turned out to be a tweaker?"

"He deserves the truth, Elliot."

"Does it matter? She's gone."

"It matters to me. I'm here because of Jill. She saved my life and Brianna's."

"I didn't leave that out. In his mind, she died trying to protect you. I just didn't say that she returned to get you out."

Rayna shook her head, then ran a hand through her hair. "But—"

Elliot was quick to jump in. "If you want to have that conversation with him, be my guest but be ready for the fallout."

"I had no way of knowing what was going to happen."

"Exactly. All he needs to know is that she died trying to protect you."

"And if Brianna says anything?"

"She won't."

"You don't know that."

Elliot exhaled hard and looked back at Jesse. "I'm going to have a word with him. Jump in, we'll head out in a few minutes."

She nodded as he walked off. Jesse was leaning against a tree, holding a rifle low in one hand and twisting an elastic band around his fingers in the other.

"Jesse."

"Five more minutes, Elliot. It's not six yet."

"I'm not rushing you."

He gave Elliot a hard a stare.

"I know you think we should have gone back and helped but it was too dangerous. There were too many unknowns."

"I know." Jesse nodded and sighed. "I just hope he hasn't got himself killed." He grimaced. "He would have been back by now."

Elliot sighed. "It wasn't easy getting out of that town even for us."

Jesse tossed the elastic band and kept staring off down the road. A flock of birds broke from the trees, soaring high over the homes. It was quiet. No gunfire. No engines. No screams.

"What if it doesn't work out?" Jesse asked.

"Then we return or make our home somewhere else. We'll deal with that when we get to it."

Jesse looked at his watch, his knee was jerking. It was either nervousness or stress.

"You wouldn't have been able to help."

"But I could have at least tried," Jesse said.

"And you might have died."

"Damon has saved my ass multiple times."

"And one day you will get to repay him," Elliot replied placing a hand on the tree.

"I hope so." He took a deep breath, looked at his watch again. "He's not coming, is he?"

Elliot breathed in the fresh morning air. "Maybe not now but he knows where we're heading."

Jesse nodded. "Yeah, he'll probably show up in Texas

looking better than ever."

They tried to remain lighthearted, but they both knew he could be lying dead in a ditch. The probability was high, and the odds were stacked against him. Jesse turned toward the truck. "Let's go then."

They returned, did a quick check to make sure everyone was accounted for and hopped in. Elliot fired up the engine. He gave Gary a quick glance. His eyes were closed. Either he was sleeping or not interested in talking. Elliot veered out of the driveway and turned south on Mirror Lake Drive. The atmosphere inside was quiet and somber as they left behind everything they'd come to know as home.

They'd only made it twenty yards down the road and had just gone over a rise when Kong started barking. Rayna cast a glance over her shoulder and had Evan pulled the window open in the rear so he could tell Kong to be quiet. Before he had a chance to do that, Kong jumped out and start bolting up the road.

"Oh God," Elliot said, groaning. "C'mon!"

"He's probably gone to collect one of his bones," Rayna said.

"I'll get him, Dad," Evan said.

"No, you wait here," he replied, putting the vehicle in park by the side of the road and pushing out. He didn't want to turn the vehicle around as it wasn't that far back to the house. Elliot jogged, calling his name.

"Kong! Hey boy, c'mon, we gotta go!"

As he made his way over the rise in the road, he squinted.

There in the distance, at the mouth of his driveway, running his hands through Kong's hair was Damon. He turned Elliot's way and a flicker of a smile appeared.

"Well, I'll be damned."

Damon made his way down to meet him, his face blackened by smoke. When he caught up with Elliot, they hugged it out. As they parted Elliot looked off down the road, an expression of concern on his face.

"Ella?" Elliot asked.

Damon dropped his chin before shaking his head.

"I'm sorry."

He nodded.

They made their way back to the truck. As soon as Jesse caught sight of him he got out of the truck and had this big grin on his face. "I knew it! Shit, I told you he would make it!"

"I know you did," Elliot said with a smile.

Damon gripped Jesse's hand and pulled him in for a pat on the back. He greeted the others and hopped into the rear, taking a seat near the window.

"Where's Jill?" he asked.

The very mention of her name stirred Gary from his slumber. He looked at Damon for a second then closed his eyes. No one needed to explain, Damon understood. That was the thing about the new world they were living in. Death lingered at their door every day. There were no guarantees that anyone would survive. As they drove away, heading for uncharted territory, Elliot tried not to dwell on what challenges or horrors lay before them since they were living on borrowed time and taking each day as it came. Instead, he glanced at his kids in the rearview mirror, and envisioned a country that would rise again from the ashes, a tomorrow where his kids would be safe, and a city they could one day call home.

.

* * *

THANK YOU FOR READING

Days of Danger: (Book 3)

Please take a second to leave a review, it's really appreciated. Thanks kindly, Jack.

A Plea

Thank you for reading Days of Danger. If you enjoyed the book, I would really appreciate it if you would consider leaving a review. Without reviews, an author's books are virtually invisible on the retail sites. It also lets me know what you liked. You can leave a review by visiting the book's page. I would greatly appreciate it. It only takes a couple of seconds.

Thank you — **Jack Hunt**

Newsletter

Thank you for buying Days of Danger, published by Direct Response Publishing.

Click here to receive special offers, bonus content, and news about new Jack Hunt's books. Sign up for the newsletter. http://www.jackhuntbooks.com/signup/

About the Author

Jack Hunt is the author of horror, sci-fi and post-apocalyptic novels. He currently has three books out in the War Buds Series, Two books in the Wild Ones series, three in the Camp Zero series, five books out in the Renegades series, three books in the Agora Virus series, one called Blackout, one called Final Impact, one called Darkest Hour, one out in the Armada series, a time travel book called Killing Time and another called Mavericks: Hunters Moon. Jack lives on the East coast of North America.

CPSIA information can be obtained
at www.ICGtesting.com
Printed in the USA
LVOW11s1325090418
572782LV00003B/203/P